A Fake Girlfriend for Chinese New Year

Holidays with the Wongs, Book 3

Jackie Lau

First edition: January 2020

Print ISBN: 978-1-989610-42-8

Editor: Latoya C. Smith, LCS Literary Services

Cover Design: Flirtation Designs

Chapter 1

Bouquet of flowers in hand, Zach Wong exited the grocery store and headed down Main Street. It was a crisp winter day in early January. The sun had shone brightly earlier, but now it was dusk and there was a cool wind off Lake Huron.

He passed the doctor's office, the dentist's office, and the pottery shop, which inexplicably had survived for a decade despite the lack of tourism in the sleepy lakeside town called Mosquito Bay. Next, there was the elementary school, the diner, the bakery, and two units that had been vacant for nearly a year.

A few people were coming out of the Tim Hortons as he walked by.

"Zach! Haven't seen you in a while." Al, a bartender at Finn's, slapped him on the back.

Zach's brothers didn't want to live in Mosquito Bay, didn't enjoy being in a community where everyone knew each other and there was only one bar, but Zach liked it here.

"I guess it's been longer than usual," Zach said. "You weren't working last Friday, right? How's the family up in Owen Sound?"

"They're doing well. My old man broke his arm, though. Fell off a ladder when he was putting up Christmas lights." Al nodded at the flowers. "Who's the lucky lady?"

Zach just smiled and shrugged.

He talked to Al for a couple minutes, then walked onward, passing Wong's Wok, the restaurant his grandparents had run for decades. A typical small-town Chinese-Canadian restaurant. The new owners weren't named Wong, but they'd kept the name, not wanting to replace the sign. There was a sheet of paper in the window that said, "Now serving pad Thai." That was new, too. There had been no pad Thai back in his grandparents' day.

Finn's was next door. Like Wong's Wok, there was no one named Finn there anymore, but the name had endured.

Zach turned off Main Street and walked by Great Lakes Bed and Breakfast. It was another five minutes before he reached his destination. Though the front door was never locked, he rang the doorbell anyway. His mother answered.

"For you," he said, handing her the bouquet as he stepped inside.

"How lovely!" Mom enveloped him in a hug. "Thanks, Zach."

"Where are my flowers?" Ah Ma, his grandmother, asked as she shuffled into the hall. "Ah, I see. They are mums for your *mum*. It is not fair that there are no flowers called ahmas. They would be a bestseller! The biggest tropical flowers. Bright pink."

"No, they'd be poisonous," Ah Yeh said, coming up behind her. "Just like your cooking."

He stepped to the side as his wife attempted to swat him.

"My cooking isn't poisonous!" Ah Ma said.

"You gave me food poisoning."

"One time, forty years ago. You are always holding that over my head."

She tried to swat Ah Yeh again, but he moved out of the way. They chased each other around the house, though it was hardly at a fast speed, as they were both close to ninety. It was more like watching two tortoises run a race.

Zach chuckled. He enjoyed being able to see his family at least once a week. His brothers, Greg and Nick, lived in Toronto and he usually only saw them at holidays. Amber, his little sister, had moved to Stratford, which was an hour away. But Zach had stayed. Well, he'd gone away for university, but he'd come back after finishing teacher's college.

"Stop it!" Dad entered the front hall. He looked at his parents and shook his head. "One of you will fall and break a hip, and that's the last thing we need."

"No, I am strong. Big muscles." Ah Ma stopped chasing her husband and attempted to flex her arm.

Dad snorted, as did Ah Yeh.

"Dinner is almost ready," Mom said. "How about you put the flowers in the vase and set the table, Zach?"

Ten minutes later, he was digging into his roast chicken, potatoes, and green beans. Sunday night dinners with his family had become a tradition in the past few years. He and his grandparents would go to his parents' house, and his mom and dad would cook. Occasionally Amber came, too.

"So, what did you do for New Year's?" Mom asked.

"Did you kiss anyone at midnight?" Ah Ma made smooching noises. "Did you go to any big parties?"

"I was at Finn's," Zach said. "Nothing exciting."

"You didn't answer my first question," Ah Ma complained.

He laughed. "No, I didn't kiss anyone."

Ah Ma shook her head. "Greg and Nick have girlfriends now. But *you*." She pointed her finger at him as though accusing him of a heinous crime. "You have not dated since Marianne, right? I keep my ears open. Nobody has said anything about you dating. We set you up with Diana, and that did not go well, but we—I mean *you*—can try again!"

Zach felt a ball of tension in his stomach as he recalled Thanksgiving. His family had decided that since Zach, Nick, Greg, and Amber were all single, it would be a great idea to set them all up on blind dates.

Although Zach's wasn't exactly a blind date, was it? He'd known Diana since childhood. Their families were friends, and Zach had been particularly good friends with Diana's older brother, Sebastian.

Regardless, it had not gone well, though Nick had made out with Greg's date and they were still together. At Christmas, Greg had convinced the family to help him make a snow fort for his high school girlfriend, and now they were a couple again, too.

Zach was happy for his brothers. If that's what they wanted, it was great.

But Zach had been in love once, and it hadn't ended well. In fact, it had ended with a diamond ring getting tossed in his face.

So, no, thank you. He wasn't interested in going through that again. Why keep doing something that brought you pain?

He'd spent many long nights at the bar, not drinking himself into oblivion, but simply because he wanted to be somewhere other than the house he'd rented with Marianne.

The one bright spot in all those late nights at Finn's? He'd become good friends with Jo.

His engagement had ended more than four years ago, but Zach remembered exactly what it had been like. He didn't need a repeat.

His family, however, seemed keen on him being in a relationship. There had been Thanksgiving's matchmaking extravaganza, and many comments since. *Oh, do you know Lizzy, who works at Tim Hortons? She's Magda's daughter, and I thought we could set you up... Wasn't Lizzy cute in her corn-cob costume at the harvest festival?*

And now, the mention of New Year's reminded him of the next big family dinner.

Chinese New Year.

Would his family try to set him up with another woman? Unfortunately, the odds seemed good. True, there were no matchmaking efforts at Christmas for Zach, but he had a feeling they were biding their time and the next family holiday would involve unwanted matchmaking for him and possibly Amber.

"What is going on, Zach?" Ah Ma asked. "You are deep in thought. It is not like you. You are acting like Greg."

"Oh, nothing," he said. "Just trying to prepare myself for work tomorrow."

He shared pleasant conversation with his family and listened to Ah Yeh describe his latest finds on Amazon.

But once dinner was over and he was walking home, he started thinking about Chinese New Year again. He couldn't bear more matchmaking with his mother's bridge partner's cousin's daughter, or the corn-cob costume lady who worked at Tim Hortons. He was happy with his life as it was. He enjoyed his job as a high school science teacher. He had lots of friends. He played in a hockey league on Monday nights. He had his family.

No, it wasn't the exciting life that Marianne had wanted, but he liked it. He didn't need a replacement for his ex-fiancée.

He did, however, need to take preventative measures to ensure he didn't have to suffer through more matchmaking at the next family holiday. Thanksgiving had been a shit show.

What would dissuade his family?

Well, the most effective thing would be if he already had a girlfriend. His family wouldn't set him up with anyone then. He didn't want a real girlfriend, but maybe he could get a fake girlfriend?

He wasn't sure where the idea had come from, but once it popped into his mind, it wouldn't leave.

A fake girlfriend would be the perfect solution to his problem. He'd bring a woman to dinner on Chinese New Year—a woman of his choosing who knew the whole thing was an act.

Zach had a bunch of female friends, but most of them were married or in relationships.

However, there was one woman who would play the role perfectly.

"What would you like?" Dr. Jo MacGregor asked. "An elephant, a horse, or a dog?"

"A dog!" Six-year-old Savannah bounced in the dentist chair.

"A pink one or a yellow one?"

"Yellow!"

Jo pumped air into the yellow balloon then twisted it into the shape of a dog. She handed it to the little girl.

Savannah frowned. "It's just like the horse you made me last time."

"Savannah!" said the girl's mother, Kyla. "What do you say when someone gives you something?"

"Thank you," Savannah said with a world-weary sigh.

The girl was right. Jo's dog was identical to her horse, but nobody had complained. Until today.

Jo suppressed a laugh.

Fortunately, she was a better dentist than balloon animal artist, but usually the kids enjoyed the balloon animals.

"If you use your imagination," Jo said, "I'm sure you can see that it's a very nice puppy."

Savannah squinted at the balloon animal. "I see it now!"

Having finished with her last patient of the day, Jo went over a few things, then returned home for a quick dinner before going out to the town's bar.

She had plans every Friday night at Finn's. It was the highlight of her week, and she'd been thinking about it all day, as she'd looked in people's mouths and filled cavities and made unimpressive balloon animals.

"Here's your Guinness." Al set a pint in front of her.

"Thank you," she murmured, then returned to staring out the window, waiting for her friend as she sat at their usual table near the front. Sometimes he was a bit late, if he stopped to chat with someone on the walk over, but never more than ten minutes.

And there he was now, wearing his blue parka, a toque pulled low over his ears. He waved at her from outside and she waved back, trying to tamp down the giddy feeling in her chest.

Really, it was embarrassing that she felt like this around him. She was a thirty-three-year-old woman, for God's sake, not a schoolgirl.

How many of his students had crushes on him? She couldn't help wondering.

"Hey," she said as he walked up to the table.

Zach Wong took off his toque, revealing his perfect dark brown hair. It was a little long and floppy, with a slight wave. Hugh Grant hair, she called it. It was unfair that his hair didn't get messed up when he put on a winter hat. Hers, on the other hand...

"Let's sit at the back today," he said. "I have something to ask you."

A handsome man was inviting her to the dark corner of the bar. Her heart beat a touch rapidly, even though she knew it didn't mean *that*.

"Sure," she said with a smile, gripping her pint as she followed him. When she was sitting down, she asked, "What is it?"

"Well," he said, "the Lunar New Year is coming up soon."

"That's in February?"

"This year, it's January twenty-fifth. I'm afraid my family is going to invite a date for me, like at Thanksgiving. So I was wondering..."

He rested his elbow on the table and leaned closer to her. She inhaled his piney scent.

Dammit, this attraction was so *inconvenient*.

She'd known Zach since they were kids, but not well—she'd been three years ahead of him in school. Then one day four years ago, they'd both been drinking away their heartbreak at the bar, and they'd bonded over their broken engagements.

They'd become friends, and two years ago, Jo had developed this inconvenient crush on Zach. Inconvenient because it was quite clear he had no interest in another relationship.

Many times, she'd told herself that she should stop meeting him for drinks, and maybe then she'd finally rid herself of these stupid feelings.

Except every week, they met at Finn's. She couldn't help herself.

She had a successful dental practice, which she'd taken over from her father after his retirement. She owned a cute little house on the edge of town. She could cook. She could garden, and she grew the best tomatoes on the block. She was pretty good at many things.

And yet...

"I want you to come to my parents' house on Chinese New Year," Zach said, "and pretend to be my girlfriend."

A burst of laughter escaped Jo's lips, and with it, unfortunately, a mouthful of dark beer. It landed on Zach's sweater.

Oh, God. She'd spit beer on Zach Wong.

"You want me...to pretend to be your girlfriend?" she asked as she grabbed a handful of napkins and started frantically dabbing at his sweater. She could feel his muscles underneath, and mmm, that was nice.

She leaned back. She should probably let him clean himself off.

"Yes," he said, "I want you to be my fake girlfriend so my family won't set me up with anyone for Chinese New Year."

"Well, there's a sentence that's never been uttered before in Mosquito Bay." Her cheeks flamed. "I'm so sorry. About the beer, I mean."

"It's no big deal." That was Zach, never fazed by anything. "So, will you do it?"

"You think your family will believe we're together?"

"Why wouldn't they?"

"Won't it be a little suspicious if you suddenly show up with a girlfriend when you haven't mentioned a girlfriend before?"

"Good point." He drummed his fingers on the table. "We'll have to go on dates in the next few weeks. Do something other than drinking at the bar every Friday. Then my parents will hear about it through the gossip vine."

"Yes!" Jo said, with perhaps a little too much enthusiasm.

She couldn't help it. Zach was asking her on a date!

True, it was a fake date, but still. Exciting times.

God, she was pathetic.

She had a sip of her beer and managed not to spit it on anyone this time, which she counted as a win.

She would be Zach's fake girlfriend; she couldn't help herself from agreeing. But while they were pretending, she must absolutely not give away her feelings, or that might be the end of their friendship. Jo had a small circle of friends, and she didn't want to lose one.

Would he want to kiss her as part of their act?

Her hands flew to her mouth.

"Are you having second thoughts?" Zach asked.

"No, it's fine. I'll do it."

"Thanks." He raised his pint, and she clinked hers against it. "I owe you."

"Yes, you do," she said good-naturedly.

They drank their beer in silence for a minute before Al came around and talked to Zach about hockey. Normally, Jo would join in, but today, she was lost in thought.

She was going to get exactly what she wanted.

Pity it would all be fake.

Chapter 2

"MORE FLOWERS FOR YOUR mother?" asked the cashier at Foodland.

"Not this time." Zach smiled at her and she flushed.

He knew his smile was powerful. It didn't make every woman drop to her knees, but when he wanted to fool around, he had little trouble finding a partner. He certainly hadn't been celibate since Marianne ended their engagement, but it wasn't like he was sleeping his way through all the single women in town.

"Who's the lucky lady?" the cashier asked.

This time, he shot her an enigmatic smile before exiting the grocery store. He had many different smiles, all for slightly different purposes.

Zach drove the short distance to Jo's house in his old Ford Focus and knocked on her door. Strangely, his heart was thumping a little quickly, like he was nervous.

But he was just spending the evening with a friend.

No, he definitely wasn't nervous. There was no reason to be.

The door opened, revealing Jo. She was wearing dark jeans and a brown sweater that hugged her curves. He'd likely seen her in this sweater before, but it looked really good on her. Her light brown hair fell in waves, and she wore silver earrings of some sort.

"You look nice," he said, swallowing.

She fidgeted with her hair. "Nobody's around now. You don't have to pretend." Her eyes lit up. "You brought me carnations. They're my favorite—how did you know?"

To be honest, Zach hadn't even known they were carnations. He'd just seen the pink flowers and figured she'd like them.

He shrugged. "Lucky guess."

"Matt never got me flowers, even though I told him exactly what I liked."

Matt was, frankly, a douche canoe. Not that Zach had ever met the man, but from the bits and pieces Jo had shared about her ex-fiancé over the years, it had become apparent that the guy had never deserved Jo.

Which was why she'd ended the engagement. Because she'd realized she deserved better.

After Jo put the flowers in the vase, Zach drove the two of them to Cardinal's, the nice-ish restaurant on the outskirts of town. The server, Jacob, a former student of Zach's who was maybe nineteen now, seated them at a table by the window and kept tripping up over the list of specials.

"We have a pizza today with fresh rainbow trout. Or sardines. I mean, anchovies. We also have ravioli stuffed with...peppers? It started with a 'p.' No, it wasn't peppers...pumpkin, maybe? Shit, I'll go check. It's my second day on the job" His face paled. "Sorry for saying 'shit.' Dammit, I did it again!"

Jo smiled at him kindly. "Don't worry. I'm going to order the mussels, no matter what the specials are."

"Oh, uh, there's a mussel special, too. Our regular mussel entrée has white wine, but I think the special one is cooked in ale?"

"Probably. They used to have that as a special every two weeks when I worked here."

"You used to work at Cardinal's, Dr. MacGregor?" the kid asked.

"Yeah, in my last year of high school. The first day, I spilled seafood marinara all over a lady from out of town who was wearing a white silk blouse."

The kid chuckled.

Zach smiled at his date trying to make their server feel more at ease. Jo wasn't as outgoing as he was, but she was good at this sort of thing.

"What would you like today, Mr. Wong?" Jacob asked.

"You can call me Zach, now that you've graduated."

Jacob looked at him as though this was a horrifying suggestion, even weirder than rainbow trout on pizza. Which surely someone had tried before, but Zach didn't like seafood on pizza.

"I couldn't call you that," Jacob sputtered. "You're Mr. Wong."

"Okay. Mr. Wong, if you prefer."

After they placed their orders, Jacob left and silence descended on the table. It was strange to be at a nice restaurant with Jo. When he saw her, it was usually at the bar.

"I find it weird being called Mr. Wong outside of school," he said.

"Yeah, I understand. I find it weird being called Dr. MacGregor outside the office. Dr. MacGregor is my father."

"For me, I think it's partly because I don't look like I should have a Chinese last name. I like my name, and people from Mosquito Bay know my family and don't question it. But students who are bussed in from other towns, other teachers...sometimes they ask, and it's awkward. Nick and Greg look more Chinese than I do. I look a bit like a white version of my dad. Does that sound strange?"

Jo considered this for a second. "I don't know what it's like, of course, but I understand what you're saying."

Occasionally, people could tell Zach wasn't entirely white from his appearance. It was awkward when people played guessing games about his background and thought it was fun.

He didn't talk about this stuff much, but there were other things he'd talked about with Jo that he didn't normally share. Although Zach had continued to act like his fun, relaxed self most of the time after his broken engagement, he'd talked to her about it a little. About his heartbreak, how he was hurt that the life he wanted was too boring and unfulfilling for Marianne, even though she'd initially been happy to move to Mosquito Bay.

Still, it was Marianne's right to feel that way, and he was glad she'd ended it before they'd started planning the wedding.

Facebook—the rare times he used it—told him that she now lived in Toronto, and she appeared to be enjoying herself there. Like Nick, she seemed to belong in the big city.

He was happy for her, but it had hurt. He'd—

"You know who you look like?" Jo asked suddenly, bringing him out of his thoughts.

"Who?"

"Keanu Reeves."

"You think I look like Keanu Reeves?"

"Yeah, a little. Did you see *Always Be My Maybe*? He was hilarious in that."

Zach shook his head.

"But you look more like Matrix-era Keanu Reeves. You don't think so?"

"That's a big compliment. I'm not sure I can accept it. Are you saying you think I'm sexy?" He waggled his eyebrows.

Jo's mouth fell open, and she paled.

Shit.

"Sorry," he said. "It's not—"

"Here's your bread and wine!" Jacob said.

Zach's red wine nearly sloshed onto the white tablecloth, but Jacob managed to catch it just in time before he scurried to another table.

Jo reached for her wine and had a gulp, then grabbed a piece of bread.

"Again, I'm sorry," Zach said. "I don't want to make you uncomfortable."

"No worries." She plastered on a smile. "It's fine."

He could tell it wasn't, but also that she didn't want to talk about it.

She took a sip of her wine—a sip, not a gulp this time—and fixed her hair.

She really did look lovely tonight, but she wasn't for him. This was pretend, and she was his friend. He wasn't sure if she was willing to give a relationship another go—she hadn't talked about that recently—but he wasn't.

His life was fine the way it was.

You think I'm sexy?

Dear God, it was a miracle Jo hadn't done more than open her mouth wide in horror.

She did think Zach was very sexy, and he looked gorgeous in the black dress shirt he was wearing tonight. He looked a bit like Keanu Reeves, it was true, but why had she felt the need to tell him that?

Zach had been playing around when he made that comment about being sexy, but could he tell the truth from how she'd reacted?

She didn't think so. Still, it had made her jittery, made her feel like maybe he could read her mind, and oh, wasn't that a horrifying thought?

But now everything was back on track. She was eating her mussels and slathering her bread with butter and dipping it in the juices, and it was all delicious. This had been her favorite meal when she'd worked here over a dozen years ago, and Cardinal's hadn't changed much over the years. They served good food, but they'd never been on the cutting edge of trends, and the dining room hadn't been updated since she was a teenager.

Across from her, Zach was cutting off a piece of his medium-rare steak, which, in her opinion, was the perfect way to cook a steak, and oh God, why did she keep finding more things to like about him?

Though she usually prided herself on being upfront and honest, her secret crush on Zach was the exception. Only Tiffany knew. Jo was determined that no one else would ever find out.

After they'd finished their meals, Jacob came over to clear their plates and recite the day's desserts. Jo really hoped today was Fudge Brownie Day.

"We have two desserts," Jacob said. "Tiramisu and fudge brownie sundae."

"Did you say fudge brownie sundae?" Jo asked. After all, Jacob had messed up the anchovy pizza special earlier.

"Yeah."

"Not just fudge brownies with whipped cream?"

"No, fudge brownie sundae. It's new. Fudge brownies with vanilla ice cream, peanut butter ice cream, whipped cream and chocolate sauce. Or fudge sauce? I don't know."

Jo wasn't quite sure what the difference between chocolate sauce and fudge sauce was, but that was a minor detail.

It sounded amazing.

Sure, it would be quite sweet and terrible for her teeth, but a woman had to have a few indulgences in life.

And sure, she could probably eat it all by herself, but she was on a "date" with Zach Wong, and sharing a fudge brownie sundae would be a very datish thing to do.

"What do you think, sweetie?" she said, the endearment popping out of her mouth before she could think about it. "Should we share it?"

"Sounds good." He turned to Jacob. "One fudge brownie sundae."

"Coming right up," Jacob said.

Once he'd left, Zach said, "If you call me 'sweetie,' what should I call you?"

"Darling." She'd dreamed of him calling her that.

"Darling it is."

They talked quietly for a few minutes, until a high voice shouted, "Dr. MacGregor!"

A little girl scampered toward their table. It was Savannah, wearing a purple party dress.

"I named my puppy Alfred," Savannah said.

Jo smiled at her. "That's a good name for a dog."

"But Alfred wants a friend. Can you make me another balloon dog now? Please?"

"I'm sorry. I don't have any balloons with me."

"Oh." Savannah twisted her mouth, then started back toward her family's table.

She'd only taken two steps before she collided with Jacob.

Who was, of course, carrying a fudge brownie sundae, cherry on top.

Jo saw it happen in slow motion.

"Zach!" she cried.

Unfortunately, there wasn't enough time for Zach to move out of the way before the fudge brownie sundae toppled off the tray. Chocolate sauce and ice cream spilled all over his hair and shirt, though he managed to catch the glass dish before it landed on his crotch.

Oh, dear.

Zach, however, quickly recovered his composure. He held out his arms, looked at his ruined shirt, and said, "Want some ice cream, darling?"

Jo sat in the passenger's seat of Zach's car as he left the parking lot. Cardinal's had quickly brought them a new sundae and comped their dessert and wine, and now their so-called date was over.

They didn't say anything for a minute or two, and then Zach started to laugh. It was a contagious sort of laughter, because soon Jo was laughing, too.

"People will definitely…be talking about our date," Zach wheezed.

"Which is exactly what you wanted."

"I didn't ask to have an ice cream sundae decorate my shirt."

"You could start a hot new trend."

"Cold trend, you mean." He glanced over at her, and her heart skipped a beat when he smiled like he didn't have a care in the world.

Whereas if Jo had been on the receiving end of the spilled ice cream, she wouldn't have been a happy camper. After all, she was wearing a nice sweater for her first date with the man she'd had a crush on for two years.

Now, one of Jo's domestic skills—along with growing great tomatoes and making really good French toast—was her ability to remove any stain. But still. Although she wouldn't have gotten angry about the spilled sundae, she might not be able to laugh about it yet.

"At least my shirt is black," Zach said. "Hey, you want to come over and watch the end of the game?"

Watching Hockey Night in Canada was something they'd occasionally do together on Saturday nights. It was part of their friendship, along with Friday nights at Finn's.

Dinner at Cardinal's, on the other hand, was something different, and Jo had enjoyed it very much, despite the unfortunate ending. Zach picking her up and handing her a bouquet of carnations—that was the stuff of her dreams.

And now they were back to Jo and Zach, friends in heartbreak.

"Sure," she said, trying to hide her disappointment.

"Better go to my place so I can get changed. I'll walk you home later."

The Leafs were winning three to two against the Bruins when Zach flipped on the television at the start of the third period. Jo curled up on the couch as he went upstairs. She tried to focus on the hockey game, rather than picturing him without a shirt, but it was a lost cause.

If only she could drizzle chocolate sauce on his bare chest, maybe garnished with cherries and whipped cream for good measure, and lick it off...

Stop it, brain! It's not going to happen.

Zach was a good friend, and he'd never shown any interest in her. There was no reason that should change now, just because they were faking a relationship.

After the game—the Leafs won—Jo still didn't want to leave.

"Let's watch *Always Be My Maybe*," she said to Zach. "Since you've never seen it and that's a travesty."

They started the movie, and though Jo very much wanted to watch it, she soon found herself getting sleepy.

Maybe she was crashing after all the sugar in that sundae. She curled up against the arm of the couch…

Something didn't feel right.

Jo opened her eyes and jolted up as she took in her surroundings.

She was on Zach's couch, covered in a fleece blanket, and sunlight was filtering through the curtains.

It was morning.

She'd spent the night at Zach's.

"Hey." Zach stepped into the living room with two cups of coffee in hand.

"What time is it?" she asked, her voice raspy.

"Nine."

"Shit, I have to get home. I'm supposed to be at my parents' house for brunch at ten, and I need to shower."

"You can shower here."

"But I need a change of clothes."

"Of course. Just drink your coffee and you can be on your way."

"No sugar?"

"No sugar. I know how you like it."

Frankly, Jo kind of liked sugar in coffee, but it wasn't necessary and she was trying to limit her sugar intake, especially after all the ice cream she'd consumed last night—that sundae hadn't exactly been small.

She took the mug from his outstretched hand and her fingers brushed against his, which was as much touching as they ever did.

"My neck hurts," she said.

"I would have moved you from the couch, but I didn't want to disturb you."

He'd thoughtfully put a blanket over her, and he'd made her coffee the way she wanted it. The only time Matt had made her coffee, it had been weak and overly sweet.

She needed to stop comparing men to Matt.

Her ex hadn't cheated on her or stolen from her or threatened her. Nor had he done any of the other things that women wrote to advice columns—or posted on Reddit—about.

She used to read those columns to convince herself that Matt was a good guy and she was lucky to have him. But then she'd noticed a pattern. Women would describe all the horrible, jaw-dropping trash their husband or boyfriend did, then end with, "He's a good guy and maybe I'm being too hard on him." Basically, "My husband kills unicorns, but he cooks dinner once a month." Women were taught to be forgiving and lower their expectations.

Whereas when men wrote in, they'd say something like, "Occasionally she eats food with raw garlic and her breath smells." Or, "She gained ten pounds and my new twenty-year-old assistant at work is hot and smiled at me once."

It was rough in the dating world. Matt wasn't the worst guy out there, true, but he'd neglected their relationship and never prioritized her, and she'd realized it was better to be single than to have what she did with him.

Jo shouldn't swoon over a cup of coffee. It was just coffee. Except she, pathetically, swooned over nearly everything Zach did.

"Thanks," she said. "Is your nosy neighbor still out working in his garage every morning?"

"He is."

"So he'll see me leave your house on a Sunday morning and draw conclusions. It'll be good for our story."

Zach's mouth curved into a stunningly attractive smile. "It will indeed."

"I hear you're dating Zach Wong," Jo's mother said over brunch a couple hours later.

Well, that was fast, though Jo couldn't say she was surprised.

"I am," she said. "Where did you hear that?"

"Shelly. She said you were at Cardinal's last night, and the waiter spilled an ice cream sundae all over Zach. How long have you been seeing him?" Mom lifted a forkful of salad to her mouth. She seemed a touch hurt that she'd had to learn about her daughter's date from Shelly Sanderson.

"Not long," Jo said. "That was our first official date." For once, she allowed herself to sound dopey and in love when talking about Zach. No acting required.

"I'm glad you're finally dating again," Becky, Jo's sister, said before dropping some quiche on the baby asleep in her arms. "Oops."

Becky was two years younger than Jo. She'd been married for more than five years and had three children; the older two were currently squishing bread rolls at the other end of the table.

"Yes, I'm glad, too," Mom said.

Jo's family had been bugging her about her love life. Not because they thought she was a failure for being single at thirty-three and having a broken engagement. It was more that they were all happily married and couldn't imagine it any other way. They meant well, but Jo's situation seemed to baffle them. Her parents had met when they were twenty; Becky and her husband had been twenty-one, in their final year of university. Dating in your thirties—in the age of Tinder and other apps—wasn't something they knew anything about.

As Jo looked around at her family, all excited to hear that she'd begun dating again, she made a resolution.

She'd spent two years in love with Zach, and he was never going to want another relationship, that much was obvious. Two years was a lot of time to waste on a man who wouldn't love her back.

Sure, there were lots of crappy men out there, and sure, Mosquito Bay wasn't a big town, but she wasn't restricted to the men in Mosquito Bay, and maybe she'd get lucky, like the other members of her family.

It was possible, wasn't it?

She would not settle, like she had with Matt. She would keep her expectations firmly intact, thank you very much, and hope she found a guy similar to Zach, but emotionally available, or whatever you called it.

She'd enjoy her "dates" with Zach Wong, but that was only temporary.

After January 25, she'd do her best to finally move on.

Chapter 3

"By the way, I have a girlfriend." Zach spoke nonchalantly as he dug into his fried rice, but he couldn't help smiling as he anticipated his family's reaction. He was at his parents' place for Sunday dinner, along with his grandparents and Amber.

Sure enough, his announcement had quite an impact.

"You do?" Ah Ma said, practically shouting.

"How wonderful," Mom said. "Who is she?"

"Jo MacGregor."

"You two have been friends for a while, haven't you?"

"Yes, and we decided...well...that we have other feelings for each other, too." He wasn't his smoothest today.

"Invite her next Sunday," Ah Ma said. "I will make her a nice meal."

Dad gave his mother a look. "You will scare her away with your horrible cooking."

"I tease! You knew I was teasing, Zach, didn't you?"

"I'm not having her over next Sunday," Zach said. "She can meet everyone at Chinese New Year the following weekend, when Greg and Nick are in town."

"Not that we haven't all met her before," Mom said, "but usually she's examining my teeth when I see her."

"I will get out my list of questions!" Ah Ma said gleefully. "Sixty-nine questions to ask future granddaughter-in-law."

Zach choked on his rice. For multiple reasons.

"What is wrong?" Ah Ma asked.

"Sixty-nine questions," Amber said. "That's, um, an awful lot."

"Sixty-nine. It is a good number, isn't it? It always makes people laugh when I say it, so I think it must be a good number."

Zach and Amber looked at each other.

"Um," Zach said.

"Do you want to tell her?" Amber asked.

"No, thank you."

"What are you not telling me?" Ah Ma demanded. "What is wrong with sixty-nine? Is it some weird sex thing?"

"I don't know if I'd say *weird*..." Dad began.

"Ah, it is a *normal* sex thing?"

"It's perfectly normal," Mom said.

Zach was having flashbacks to the sex-ed talks his parents had given him when he was a preteen. He supposed he was grateful for those, but he didn't really want to think about that now.

"In fact," Mom continued, "Amber came home from school one day—I think she was eleven—and asked me what it was."

Everyone looked at Amber, and Zach couldn't help smirking, just a tiny bit, at his sister's discomfort.

"You told her?" Ah Ma said. "Why won't you tell me?"

"You can look it up on the internet," Dad said.

"I don't know how to use the internet."

"I do," said Ah Yeh, who had been silent up until this point.

"All you know how to do is order things we don't need. You know what arrived yesterday?" Ah Ma pointed at her husband but looked at her son. "An avocado slicer, an egg slicer, and a cake decorating set. Why do we need those things? He doesn't even like boiled eggs. Or cake."

"I like cake." Ah Yeh crossed his arms over his chest. "I just don't like that dry vanilla cake you buy from the grocery store."

"Wah, that is the best. So cheap!" Ah Ma said. "But this is just a distraction from my question. What is sixty-nine? I don't want to use the internet to find out."

"Yeah, maybe it's best you don't use the internet for that." Dad looked pointedly at Ah Yeh. "You might find porn, and I don't want to have to fix your computer because you got a virus from looking at porn again."

"I don't know what you are talking about," Ah Yeh said.

On the plus side, no one was talking about Zach marrying Jo now—Ah Ma's comment about her being a "future daughter-in-law" was the main reason he'd choked on his rice.

But when he got home, he'd have to scrub this conversation from his brain.

Tuesday evening, Zach sat in Wong's Wok, waiting for Jo to arrive.

The reason for this choice in venue was simple: the new owners of Wong's Wok—though Zach should probably stop thinking of them as "new," seeing as they'd run the place for twenty years—were friends with his family, and they would almost certainly tell his parents or grandparents that Zach had been here with Jo. Though he'd already told his family about his "girlfriend," they hadn't heard it from any other source—surprisingly, no one had told them about the ice cream sundae incident. This would make it look more real.

Jo walked into the restaurant a few minutes later. She removed her winter coat and toque, then sat across the table from him and smiled.

For a moment, Zach was unable to speak. He was transfixed by her smile. Good advertising for a dentist to have a nice smile, he supposed.

Then he moved his gaze lower. She was wearing a sweater that graded from light blue at the top to dark blue at the bottom. It showed more cleavage than her usual clothes, and those buttons sure were tempting.

Stop it, Zach.

He would not ogle his friend.

"Hey," he said at last, trying to sound casual.

"Hey, Zach. How's your week been?"

"A bit rough waking up for early morning basketball practice." He coached the senior boys' team. "And..."

Why couldn't he find his words? This wasn't like him.

But Jo really did look good today. She'd looked good on Saturday, too, but he hadn't found himself stunned into silence.

What was wrong with him? He'd seen her many, many times over the past few years. Why was it different now that they were supposedly in a relationship? They'd both known it was fake from the start.

He shook his head to clear it, then looked around the restaurant. There were red lanterns and other decorations on the walls for the upcoming holiday.

"Should I bring anything when I come to your parents' house for Chinese New Year?" Jo asked. "The red envelopes—how do they work? I'm sure I could get some online."

Zach wasn't sure how most people celebrated Chinese New Year, since he knew so few people of Chinese descent. He didn't know which things his family did were "normal" and which were just his family—other than Pictionary—and what would vary depending on where you were from in China.

He felt like he should be aware of these things, but he'd grown up in a small town where more than ninety-five percent of the people were white, like Jo. His father had spent most of his life in the same small town.

"You don't have to bring red envelopes," he said. "They contain money, and they're given to the younger generation. My grandparents and parents give them to us. I don't know when we'll become old enough for that to stop, but it hasn't happened yet, and none of my siblings have kids."

"Okay," Jo said. "Is there anything I can bring food-wise?"

He shook his head. "You don't need to."

"I feel like I should."

"Some fruit, if you like, but it's not a big deal, don't worry."

"I want to make a good impression on my fake prospective in-laws." She smiled at him again, and he felt a strange jittery sensation in his stomach.

He reached forward and took her hand in his. "Thank you for doing this. I know it's a hassle."

"It's not a hassle to occasionally have dinner together and accompany you to a family event."

He always felt comfortable with Jo, content when they were together. Not that anyone would notice the difference when he was with her, since that was the sort of image he always projected; it was what people expected of him.

But sometimes, that image was a bit of an act.

With her, though, it never was.

"Zachary!" Mrs. Tan came over to their table. "Long time since you came here."

Zach felt a touch of guilt. He came to the restaurant maybe once a month, though perhaps it had been two months now.

"Dr. MacGregor." Mrs. Tan smiled at Jo. "I have appointment next week. Hope I have flossed enough! Are you two..." Her gaze traveled from Jo to Zach, then down to the table, where his hand was still covering hers.

Huh. He'd completely forgotten about that, as though it felt natural to hold her hand.

"Yes," Jo said, beaming at Mrs. Tan before shooting him a lovesick gaze. She really was a good actor. He hadn't expected that of her.

Zach ordered egg rolls and chow mein; Jo ordered ginger beef.

"It's been my favorite since I was little," she told him after Mrs. Tan left. "I've never seen it at another Chinese restaurant."

"It was added to the menu in nineteen seventy-eight," he said. "After The Trip."

"The Trip?"

Apparently he'd never told her about this before. "The restaurant was open six days a week from the time my grandparents came here in the mid-sixties. They'd never taken more than two days off until The Trip—it was the only family vacation they had after moving to Canada."

Zach had heard tales of The Trip many, many times. From his grandparents, his father, and his aunt. Everyone remembered it a little differently, and they'd regularly reminisce about it at family meals. At some point he'd become sick of hearing about it—couldn't his family think of any other stories to tell?—but he smiled at the thought of telling Jo.

"For years, Ah Yeh planned this trip," he said. "A cross-country road trip out to Alberta. He'd seen pictures of Lake Louise in a magazine once, and he'd wanted to go to Banff ever since. Along the way, he planned to stop at every Chinese restaurant he could find. Research, he said. He called it a business trip, which made Dad and Aunt Cheryl roll their eyes. Anyway, in nineteen seventy-eight, before my father's final year of high school, they closed down the restaurant for a full month and finally went. Ginger beef was on the menu at many of the Chinese restaurants in the Prairies, and it seemed popular. Ah Yeh talked to the owners at every restaurant. They were usually happy to chat with someone else who was Chinese, and he convinced one of the cooks to show him how to make it. My grandpa did the cooking at Wong's Wok—my grandma is terrible in the kitchen, and she ran the front of the restaurant."

"Is ginger beef from a particular region in China?"

Zach shook his head. "It was supposedly invented at the Silver Inn in Alberta in nineteen seventy-three. A Chinese-Canadian dish."

"So it's not authentic?"

"Don't get my grandfather started on 'authenticity,'" Zach said. "These small-town Chinese restaurants in North America are kind of their own type of cuisine, adapted to fit the tastes of the people in the area. Egg rolls,

General Tso's chicken, and such. In the Prairies, they have ginger beef, and in Thunder Bay, they have a rib dish. My grandparents put that on the menu, too, but I think the Tans took them off. In Newfoundland—my grandparents went there after they retired—chow mein is made with cabbage because it used to be difficult to get the noodles there, so they had to make changes."

It was interesting how these immigrant families, many with limited English skills, had managed to make these businesses survive. Though whenever his dad talked about The Trip, he sounded like a cool teenager who didn't want to be trapped in a van with his family for half his summer vacation. Zach's father had recently started dating his mother, and they'd been devastated at the thought of spending the summer apart.

"So, yeah," Zach said. "That's why there's ginger beef on the menu."

"Were your grandparents upset that neither of their children wanted to take over the family business?"

"They encouraged my dad and my aunt to go to university, to get good degrees so they wouldn't have to work at a restaurant. Running Wong's Wok was hard work—they were *always* there, except for that one trip out west. Still, I think they were a little disappointed they had to sell the restaurant out of the family, even if they never said so." His father was a pharmacist, and Aunt Cheryl worked in finance on the other side of the country.

Their food arrived a few minutes later, and Zach didn't immediately take a bite. Instead, he watched as Jo speared a piece of deep-fried beef, covered in dark sauce, with her fork and popped it into her mouth.

"Mmm," she said, and for some reason, it made blood rush to his cock.

What was wrong with him? It was just Jo eating. Nothing special.

A drop of sauce clung to the corner of her lip. He was about to reach over to wipe it off, then decided that would be too intimate. He pointed to the corner of his own mouth. "You have some sauce...there."

She swiped at the other corner of her mouth.

"No, on your left side."

She swiped the sauce off and wiped it on her napkin, but he wished he'd gotten a chance to suck it off her finger instead. His body didn't seem to have gotten the message that this relationship was fake. He needed to have a few words with it in his stern teacher voice.

"Thank you for telling me the history of it," she said. "I never knew." Then she got a gleam in her eye. Why, it was almost a *wicked* gleam—which wasn't like Jo at all. "Can you make this for me at home, sweetie? Afterward, I'll..." She gave him a suggestive wink.

She was just playing around, acting the part. But his body responded nonetheless.

"I'll ask my grandfather to teach me," he said hoarsely. "Just for you, *darling*." He emphasized the last word as Mrs. Tan walked by.

"Everything good?" Mrs. Tan asked.

"Delicious, thank you." Jo smiled.

"Ungh," Zach said. "I mean, it's delicious."

"You haven't started eating," Jo pointed out.

"Yes, but I know it's going to be delicious."

He finally had a bite, and it was, indeed, good. He and Jo ate in companionable silence for a while, and then she mentioned the Leafs. It was the sort of thing they'd usually talk about. There were no wicked gleams or winks.

When Mrs. Tan brought out the bill with two fortune cookies on top, Zach reached for it before Jo could.

"I'm paying," he said.

"No, you paid last time."

Before he knew what was happening, Jo had grabbed the bill. She took out her credit card and held it out to Mrs. Tan.

"I insist," Jo said, turning back to him.

Well, he supposed he could allow her this, even though he really ought to be paying because he was the one who'd roped her into this fake relationship.

After Mrs. Tan left, they each took a fortune cookie. Zach opened up the package, snapped the cookie in half, and pulled out the fortunes. Plural.

"I got two." He and his siblings had considered that good luck back in the day.

The first fortune: *You will find romance in unexpected places. Lucky numbers: 7, 10, 28, 63, 45*

"What does it say?" Jo asked.

He shifted the small slip of paper to the middle of the table and turned it around. Jo leaned closer. Her hair smelled faintly of vanilla, and he wanted to bury his head in it.

Probably that fortune was getting to his mind.

The second fortune said: *Don't be stupid. Lucky numbers: 18, 23, 2, 78, 6.*

What did it all mean? That he would find love somewhere unexpected—frankly any kind of love and romance would be unexpected at this point—and he shouldn't be stupid about it? Or would it be stupid if he found romance in an unexpected place?

Well, in truth, it would be stupid to pay attention to the fortunes in a cookie.

He popped half the cookie in his mouth as Jo opened hers up. When she read her message, her eyebrows shot up, and then she started laughing.

"What is it?" he asked.

She held up the fortune so he could read it.

Brush your teeth. Lucky numbers: 69, 23, 45, 1, 15.

Zach couldn't help the strangled noise that escaped his throat when he saw the number 69, recalling the conversation with his family, then quickly pushed it out of his mind and focused on the first part of the fortune.

"It's like the fortune cookie gods know I'm a dentist," Jo said. "Terrifying, isn't it?"

"Or maybe they could tell that you haven't been brushing your teeth."

She looked affronted. "Of course I brush my teeth. How dare you!"

After tossing her fortune on her plate, Jo ate her cookie, and Zach found himself staring at her mouth again.

Hmm. This really would be an unexpected place to find romance...

He quickly dismissed the thought.

"You and Jo MacGregor, eh?" Shawn Little walked into the room where Zach taught grade ten science at the end of the day. The students had just filed out the door, and Zach was tidying up a few things.

Shawn taught phys ed and health. He was Zach's closest friend at Mosquito Bay Secondary School, and Zach had planned to tell him the truth. Just Shawn, no one else.

He beckoned his friend closer to the lab counter.

"It's a ruse," Zach said. "We're pretending we're together so my parents and grandparents don't get up to more matchmaking, especially with Chinese New Year approaching."

Shawn lifted his eyebrows. "You went to all the effort of getting a fake girlfriend to avoid their matchmaking plans?"

"I don't think you understand how annoying it can be."

"Well, no. My mom comments about my single status, but I can't say I have any experience with my family finding me a surprise date for Thanksgiving." Shawn slapped Zach on the back. "I hear your neighbor saw Jo sneaking out of your house the other morning. Are there any benefits to this fake relationship?"

"No," Zach said, rather harshly.

Though he was now thinking about him and Jo in bed together, much to his annoyance.

Don't be stupid.

That's what his fortune cookie had told him, and it was good advice, even if it had come from a questionable source.

Zach would not be stupid.

Chapter 4

Jo walked into Finn's and sat at her usual table. She waved at Becky, who was by the bar with a group of friends, and then a minute later, Al came over with a pint of Guinness.

"Waiting for your boyfriend?" he asked.

"No, I..." Jo began.

I don't have a boyfriend.

Except as far as everyone knew, she *did* have a boyfriend, a boyfriend she was very much in love with.

Too bad it was one-sided.

"Zach will be here soon," she said with a smile.

"You two have been friends for a long time," Al said. "What happened? What changed?"

Good question. Jo and Zach had never discussed their how-we-started-dating story.

"It began last Friday," she said, having no idea where she was going with this. "After we left Finn's, he walked me home, and it started snowing..."

"...and you know when you suddenly see someone in a new way?" Zach came up behind her and put his hand on her shoulder. "Well, to be honest, that had never happened to me until last week. Jo looked so pretty, snowflakes in her eyelashes, and before I knew what was happening, we were kissing."

Oh, if only.

If only they had kissed. If only he could see her differently.

Al brought Zach his usual beer. Zach held up his pint, and Jo clinked hers against his.

"Cheers to us," Zach said as he took a seat.

Jo attempted a smile, but based on Zach's concerned expression, she hadn't succeeded.

"What's wrong?" he asked, once Al had walked away.

She couldn't tell him the truth, but he was her friend, and perhaps she could tell him part of the truth. "I didn't want another relationship after I dumped Matt—"

"He wasn't good enough for you. I'm glad you dumped that asshole."

The corners of her mouth quirked up. "I'm glad, too. But lately, I've been thinking that I'd like to date again."

Zach looked at her over his pint of beer, not at all distracted by the Friday night noise of the bar, the laughter from the pool tables at the back.

She liked how he could make her feel like she was all that mattered.

"It's hard, though," she said. "There aren't a lot of options in Mosquito Bay. I could use a dating app and try to find someone in one of the nearby towns, but..."

But I'm in love with you, and I don't know how to move on.

She would, though. Somehow, after Chinese New Year, she'd try again. She'd put aside this pathetic crush on Zach and do her best. Or maybe she'd have to go on dates with other men even if she still had a crush on him, and *that* would help her move on.

"I know it's silly," she continued, the words pouring out of her now. Quietly, though; she didn't want anyone to overhear. "But Becky was always the pretty sister, the one everyone loved. The one who always had a boyfriend. I was the smart one, the athletic one, though some people told me that I could stand to lose a few pounds. And sometimes, I was envious. Then I felt guilty. I knew I should love myself as I am, but I struggled with that when I was with Matt. I thought I couldn't expect any better than a guy who didn't mind having me around."

Zach shook his head. "You deserve much more than that."

She nodded. She shouldn't be insecure, but probably most women felt this way at some point, right?

"Say it," Zach said. "'I deserve so much more than that good-for-nothing douche canoe.'"

"Douche canoe? What does that even mean?"

"That a bag isn't big enough to contain the guy, so a canoe is needed?"

She snorted. "You're making this up."

"No, it's a thing people say, I promise."

"I don't know if I'd call Matt a douchebag—or canoe. He was just…"

"As useful and affectionate as a potted fern?"

"Yeah, something like that. He wasn't evil; he just put me at the bottom of his priority list."

"Douche canoe," Zach said solemnly. "And I will always be here so you can rant about the not-so-fantastic guys you meet online, but I'm sure you'll find the right guy eventually."

Why can't you be the right guy?

"You don't want to try again, right?" she said.

"Nah, I like my life the way it is."

"You don't believe in love for yourself?"

"I don't know what I believe, but it's not something I'm looking for. If you want it, though, I want you to have it."

Oh, God. It had been a mistake to have this conversation with Zach. This was too much.

"And just so you know…" Gently, he slid his hand up her cheek and into her hair. His large hand caressed her; she could melt into his touch.

"You're very pretty, and I hope you find romance in unexpected places."

His eyes were focused intently on hers, and though he looked serious, there was still the unruly lock of hair over his forehead, the hint of a smile at his lips. He was looking at her in a way he'd never looked at her before, but he was still *Zach*, and she yearned to be with him.

Maybe he wanted her a little, too.

Wishful thinking… Or was it?

Her heart was hammering in her chest, and somehow, it felt like it was connected to his. She leaned forward and—

"Dr. MacGregor, hiiii!"

A young woman stumbled into Jo. Jo reached out her hands to steady her and tried not to curse at the interruption.

"Hey, Kyla," Zach said easily, as though he hadn't been about to kiss Jo. "Having a good night?"

"These sure are strong. Or maybe it's because I hardly drink anymore. My tolerance isn't what it used to be before Savannah was born." Kyla held up her drink, and a little sloshed over the edge of the glass.

"Let me get that for you." Zach wiped the glass with a napkin.

"Thank you!" Kyla touched his shoulder—she seemed to be an affectionate drunk. "I'm sorry about what happened at Cardinal's. I told Savannah, *no running in restaurants...*"

He laughed it off. "It didn't hurt, and the stain came out. It's all good."

"But it was your first date, wasn't it?"

"And now we have a memorable story."

"You can tell it to your children," Kyla said with a hiccup.

Becky—she'd been in the same year in school as Kyla—came over and put her hand on her friend's shoulder. "Let's order fries. I think you need some food."

"Poutine! We should have poutine." Kyla turned to Jo. "My ex has Savannah for the first Friday night in months, and I'm going to have fun!"

Becky smiled. "I'll let you get back to your date, Jo."

Zach placed a hand on Jo's knee—and Becky definitely noticed—before he held his other hand up in a wave as Becky and Kyla walked away.

"Sorry," he said suddenly, removing his hand from her knee. "Was it okay that I touched you? Both now and a few minutes ago when I touched your hair?"

"I'm your girlfriend," Jo said. "Of course you can touch me."

"I don't have to. I can lean in close, whisper in your ear..." And then he did just that, his voice soft and low. "I can make it look like we're intimate without physical contact, if you prefer."

Well, she liked this whispering business, but she liked the touching, too.

If only Kyla hadn't interrupted them.

"Zach," she said, "you were about to kiss me, weren't you?"

He scratched the back of his neck. "Uh, yeah. As part of our act."

Her heart deflated, though she wasn't completely convinced he was being honest.

"I won't do it again," he said.

She hoped that wasn't true.

Chapter 5

WHAT AM I DOING?

Zach backed his car out of the garage on Sunday morning and drove along the quiet streets to Jo's house on the other side of town.

There was a new skating trail through the woods, about forty minutes north of Mosquito Bay. Usually Zach only skated when he was playing hockey, but the idea of skating on something more than sixty meters long was appealing. The whole track was over a kilometer, which sounded nice. And romantic.

And so he'd asked Jo to go with him this morning, and she'd agreed.

Part of our act, he told himself.

Except this was different from going to Wong's Wok or Cardinal's, where they'd inevitably run into other residents of Mosquito Bay. It was possible they'd encounter no one they knew on this excursion.

You just want to see her again.

Well, they were friends. Wasn't that reasonable?

But you saw her on Friday night, and you usually only see each other once a week.

He told himself that he was just trying to get into the role.

Zach wasn't in the habit of lying to himself, however, and in truth, he'd felt like there had been a spark between them the last two times they'd met up. His hands tightened on the steering wheel as he remembered sliding his hand over her cheek.

He couldn't help himself; he wanted to do that again.

He pulled up to Jo's house, and she scampered out the door and into the passenger's seat.

"Hey." She was wearing a white toque and her usual blue parka, and she grinned at him.

He couldn't help returning her smile.

They started driving north. It had snowed yesterday morning, and sunlight reflected off the snowy fields, but the roads had been cleared. A cold day—well below freezing and a bit windy.

"You been to this place before?" Jo asked.

He glanced at her. Her brown eyes held excitement, even though they were simply going skating, something they'd both done many times before.

"No," he said, "but I thought it would be the perfect thing to do with my girlfriend."

They arrived at the skating trail around ten thirty and paid the rink attendant. Based on the lack of cars in the parking lot, it appeared they were alone. Probably had something to do with the bitterly cold weather.

They laced up their hockey skates in the little hut. It wasn't heated, but at least it offered protection from the wind.

Jo got her skates on first and tossed an "I'll race you" over her shoulder before she pushed open the door to the hut.

Zach finished tying up his skates in a hurry and followed her out. She was already whipping down the ice in long, smooth strokes, and he had lots of distance to make up.

That was no surprise. He'd played hockey with Jo; he knew she was an excellent skater.

As it turned out, he couldn't catch her. He managed to get close at one point, but then she whizzed past him, and when he reached the beginning of the trail, she was waiting for him.

"I win!" Her cheeks were pink and her toque was slightly askew, and it was just the two of them...and hell, she looked good.

Usually, Zach was a talker, but right now, he didn't talk.

He took Jo's gloved hand and raised his eyebrows. She nodded before she started skating again, not quite as fast as before, and he skated with her, holding hands.

It was a novelty, skating through the forest like this. The bare branches of the deciduous trees and the green of the conifers were covered in a layer of fluffy snow. Large flakes of snow started falling slowly from the sky, and Jo tipped her head up and smiled.

It was peaceful.

They kept skating, hand in hand, around the track.

He remembered what she'd told him the other night, about wanting another relationship, even after all that had happened.

He hoped she'd get what she wanted. He was her friend after all.

But dammit, if some part of him didn't tense at the thought of her skating hand in hand with another man.

It had been a long time since he'd felt like this.

After the fifth loop, Jo came to a stop near the hut. She was about to step through the doorway, but he took her hands and pulled her close, as if in a trance.

Once again, he raised his eyebrows, and once again, she nodded.

He kissed her.

Her mouth was welcoming, hot compared to the air around them. She curved her arms around him and pulled him even closer. It was fortunate that she was only a couple inches shorter than him, or they wouldn't have been able to make this work.

And boy, was it ever working.

She moaned softly as he took her mouth in his again and again, and when she slipped her tongue between his lips, he nearly swore.

But he didn't, because he didn't want to break the spell they were under.

He touched his tongue to hers; she felt so *necessary* right now, just as necessary as the winter clothes that were protecting them from the cold.

Suddenly, after years of friendship, kissing her was just what he needed.

A snowflake fell on her nose; he licked it off before returning to pleasuring her mouth, each of her precious sighs making his pants a little more uncomfortable.

She leaned into him, and then, suddenly, she was gone.

He caught her before she fell onto the ice.

"Perhaps we should take off our skates," she said, leading him into the hut.

She sat down on a bench and unlaced her skates. After she put her boots on, she took off her toque and unzipped her jacket, exposing her Leafs sweatshirt. Her cheeks were flushed and her hair was wild, some of it slicked with sweat, and he'd never seen anything more beautiful.

Once he'd changed into his boots, she slid across the bench, straddled him, and went right back to kissing him.

Jo was a steady presence in his life, and he'd never imagined she'd be so passionate.

His imagination clearly needed work.

Zach slid his hands under her sweatshirt and T-shirt, and he groaned as he touched her hot skin.

"Okay?" he murmured.

When she nodded, he moved his hands higher, under her sports bra.

This time, she was the one who groaned, and that sent a bolt of lust straight to his cock.

He circled her nipple with his thumb, then tweaked it. She groaned once more, and God, he wanted to hear that sound again and again.

He kissed her neck and cold cheek before making his way back to her mouth. Her sweet mouth would feel so good on—

"Daddy, what are they *doing*?"

Jo scrambled off his lap and fell backward onto the ground, landing on her ass.

"Shit, are you okay?" Zach extended a hand, realizing belatedly that he'd sworn in front of a small kid. Actually, three small children, who were all peering at him curiously.

"They were kissing, you dumb-dumb!" said Kid 2.

"You said a mean word!" said Kid 1.

Zach grabbed Jo's hand and pulled her up, and they scurried out of the hut before they could hear any more.

Once they were sitting in the safety of the car, she glanced out the window and said, "I'm sorry. I shouldn't have...you know."

He took her chin in his hand and turned her so she was looking at him. "Yes, you should have. I enjoyed it."

She gave him a tentative smile, but it wasn't enough for him, so he kissed her again, in a way that would totally scandalize those children and their parents.

"Don't apologize," he said, then started the car.

They didn't talk much on the drive back to Mosquito Bay. Zach was still trying to wrap his mind around what had happened.

He didn't understand it. He'd never wanted to kiss Jo until they'd started this charade.

He shook his head. It was probably just because he hadn't had sex in six months, and he was horny.

Really, that's all it was. And he wouldn't let anything come of it. She was his friend, and that would make things weird.

Jo sat at the back of the bakery with her hot chocolate and scone...and a wide grin on her face.

A few minutes later, her friend Tiffany walked in, her two-month-old baby in a carrier.

"So, what's up?" Tiffany asked, sitting across from Jo. "What's this emergency that required me to leave the warmth of my house?"

"I don't understand why you're complaining," Jo said. "You're having a currant scone. Isn't that worth a little trek outside?"

"It's pretty freaking cold out there." Tiffany bounced her sleeping child up and down.

Tiffany and Jo had been friends since elementary school. Their friend group used to be bigger, but the other three women had moved away from Mosquito Bay and only came back to visit family a few times a year, so usually it was just the two of them.

"You'll never guess what happened," Jo said. "We kissed!"

"You and Zach?"

"Who else could I possibly be talking about?"

Tiffany wasn't a fan of Jo's crush on Zach. Not that she disliked him, but she didn't like the idea of pining in secret for someone for years.

"Who kissed who?" Tiffany asked.

"The first time, he did, but the second time, I made the move." Jo flushed as she thought of Zach's hand on her breast...then flushed in embarrassment as she recalled how they'd been interrupted. "We went to the skating trail near Goderich. The first lap, we raced and I won."

"His delicate male ego wasn't bothered?"

"Zach doesn't have a delicate ego," Jo said. "Afterward, he took my hand and we skated together for a while." She couldn't help the smile that came to her face. "Then we kissed."

"I'm guessing by your expression that it lived up to your expectations?"

"Yes."

Oh boy, had it ever.

"I'm impressed," Tiffany said. "I figured it couldn't possibly be that good."

"I think something might actually come of this," Jo said. "Perhaps this fake relationship was just what he needed to see me in a different light."

"Jo, I love you, but I don't think it means anything. Zach's kissed many women. It's not like he's restrained himself since Marianne left him. And he never ended up dating any of those women, did he?"

The hot chocolate tasted bitter in Jo's mouth.

"Sure, he might be attracted to you," Tiffany continued, "but I doubt anything will come of it. I'm sorry, but I don't. You know he has no interest in another relationship—he's told you that."

Jo wasn't surprised by Tiffany's words. Her friend was always the pessimist. Maybe Tiffany wasn't the person Jo should have texted the instant she stepped out of Zach's car.

Or maybe she'd done it instinctively out of self-preservation, like a part of her had wanted someone to knock some sense into her.

But was what Tiffany saying really *sense*?

Tiffany wasn't the one who'd been kissed by Zach Wong. Tiffany hadn't skated through the snowy woods with him, hand in hand.

It had felt like it was more than just physical.

Jo wasn't delusional, was she?

Chapter 6

It was Chinese New Year at last. The whole reason Zach had gotten a fake girlfriend.

His siblings hadn't arrived yet, and right now, Zach and Ah Yeh were in the kitchen of his parents' house, preparing their evening feast. They would have a whole chicken and a whole fish, as they always did at Chinese New Year, plus noodles and fried rice and turnip cakes. For most holidays, his parents did the cooking, but Ah Yeh was always in charge for Chinese New Year.

Ah Ma was also in the kitchen, sitting at the table, eating the sweet rice cake made of glutinous rice flour and brown sugar.

"Aiyah," Ah Yeh said. "You will eat it all before everyone is here."

"I know. I am so sneaky!" Ah Ma said.

"I don't think 'sneaky' is the right word." Dad sat down beside his mother and helped himself to a piece of cake.

Zach hoped Jo enjoyed herself. He was suddenly nervous about the whole thing. Would she be weirded out by the chicken feet and head?

Would his grandmother really ask her sixty-nine questions?

"This year is very exciting," Ah Ma said. "All grandsons have a date! Last year, there were no girlfriends, and now, there are three. Maybe next year, all three of you will have wives."

Zach stared at her.

"What?" Ah Ma said. "You are not thinking about marriage?"

"Jo and I have been together for two weeks," Zach said. "It's a bit soon."

"But you have known each other for a long time. I think it's not too soon."

"Please don't scare her away," Mom said, walking into the kitchen.

"I am not scary!" Ah Ma said, affronted.

Dad snorted.

Zach put down his knife and turned to his grandfather. "Could you show me how to make ginger beef sometime? It's Jo's favorite."

"Ah, how sweet," Ah Ma said. "He is cooking for her. Very romantic."

Ah Yeh was focused on something on the stove, but he nodded, and Zach told himself that he'd asked about the ginger beef only because it was part of his act.

Jo stood on the doorstep to Zach's parents' house and took a few deep breaths.

This was it. The family dinner.

She wanted to make a good impression on Zach's family, especially since now, there was a real chance...

Well, Tiffany didn't think so, but Jo couldn't completely give up hope.

She hadn't wanted to show up empty-handed, so she'd brought persimmons, having learned that it was a fruit some people ate for Chinese New Year. She'd bought them on her monthly trip into London.

At last, she knocked on the door, and a moment later it swung open.

"Hey." Zach smiled at her.

His hair flopped over his forehead, and she reached up to push it to the side before kissing him on the cheek.

Just acting like his girlfriend, nothing more.

But after that chaste kiss, she couldn't help thinking about the not-so-chaste kiss by the skating rink, and her cheeks turned pink.

He smiled at her again, as though knowing exactly what was going through her mind.

A minute later, all of Zach's family had crowded into the front hall, and he introduced them. "These are my grandparents. My parents, Rosemary and Stuart. My sister, Amber. Nick and his girlfriend Lily, Greg and his girlfriend Tasha."

"It's so nice to meet you all," Jo said. "I mean, to see you again. I've met most of you before. Small town, you know."

Did she sound nervous?

She was pretty sure she sounded nervous.

"I brought persimmons." She held up the small box.

"Ah, good, good!" Ah Ma said. "I like persimmons."

Stuart picked one up. "They're not ripe yet."

"When they're not ripe, they make your mouth feel fuzzy," Greg said. "This is due to the tannins."

Oh. Jo had no idea when persimmons were ready to eat.

"No big deal," Zach said, putting his hand on her shoulder. "They'll be good in a few days. Come in and try some of the nin gou. Chinese New Year cake."

He took her hand, and she couldn't help smiling at the gesture. When they reached the dining room, he picked up a brown rectangle and held it in front of her lips.

Zach was going to feed her. And his grandmother, mother, and sister were looking on.

She took a small bite. It was chewy and not quite what she'd expected, but it wasn't unpleasant. She took a couple more bites and decided it was pretty good, now that she was accustomed to it.

"My husband made it," Ah Ma said. "Am very lucky to have husband who is a good cook. Zach wants to learn to make his ginger beef. Apparently it is your favorite?"

"Ah Ma!" Zach said. "That was supposed to be a surprise for Valentine's Day."

"Ah, sorry. Me and my big mouth."

Jo took another bite of the cake from Zach's fingers.

"Ugh, get a room," Amber said. "I can't believe all of you are coupled up now."

"Perhaps a date for you will arrive any minute," Zach said. "There's still time."

Mom shook her head. "I promised Amber we wouldn't set her up with anyone tonight, but maybe we'll find someone for Easter."

"Oh, God, *no*." Amber glared at her.

Zach fed Jo the last of the cake before planting a quick kiss on her lips.

"Woo-hoo!" Ah Ma said. "You are practicing for wedding ceremony?"

"Alright, that's enough," Zach said. "Now, Jo, I forgot to warn you about an important New Year's tradition in our family. Pictionary."

Jo couldn't help but laugh.

"Usually Amber and I are a team," he continued, "and Greg and Nick are a team. But I think you and I should be a team tonight. Amber's drawing abilities leave a little to be desired."

Amber stuck out her tongue. "I guess I'm the odd one out, since I'm the only one who's not in a couple. I can be the judge."

"You're just glad you don't have to draw anything," Nick said.

"We will kick everyone's ass." Ah Ma lifted her foot and kicked the air. She wobbled, and Stuart caught her.

"Unlikely," Ah Yeh said. "You are terrible at Pictionary."

"I am the best artist! It's not my fault you are so bad at understanding my drawings."

"Your elephant looked like a bear. How could anyone guess that?"

They kept arguing about their Pictionary skills, and Jo was glad that everyone seemed comfortable enough to act like themselves around her. She could totally handle Pictionary. She hadn't played in years, but it sounded like fun.

Zach dragged her into the hallway and rested his hands on her hips.

"How's it going?" he whispered. "You okay? Is it overwhelming?"

"No," she said, allowing herself to wrap her arms around his neck. "It's great."

I only wish it were real.

Dinner was delicious. Jo particularly liked the chicken, plus the turnip cake, which was actually made with a type of radish.

Ah Yeh allowed her to try one of the fish cheeks, which were his favorite; supposedly it was a delicacy. Jo didn't quite understand the appeal, but she didn't dislike it.

After dinner, Zach and Nick cleared the table and brought out more of the nin gou, plus Nanaimo bars, butter tarts, oatmeal cookies, and White Rabbit candies. Zach handed one of them to Jo.

"The rice paper wrapper is edible," he said.

The candy looked a bit like a white Tootsie roll. She popped it in her mouth and quite enjoyed it.

Ah Ma handed out red envelopes to her grandchildren, as well as Lily, Tasha, and Jo. She clucked her tongue as she did so.

"I hope next year there will be no red envelopes. You are all getting too old for this."

"We told you," Nick said. "You don't have to give us money."

"Yeah, you live in a penthouse in downtown Toronto. Why do you need ten dollars?" Stuart said, but he handed an envelope to Nick all the same.

"Younger generation gets red envelopes until they are married." Ah Ma looked at her grandchildren. "I hope next year, everyone is married, and there will be no red envelopes. Except maybe for a baby?"

"You know," Amber said, "we might not all get married."

"Fine. I will stop when you turn thirty-five. Greg, this is your last year."

Greg nodded his head with a grunt.

Jo regarded her envelope, red with gold lettering—not that she could read what the Chinese characters said—and a gold rat, since it was the year of the rat.

"Thank you," she said to Zach's grandmother.

"You will come back next year?"

"I hope so."

"You might change your mind after Pictionary," Amber said.

Pictionary turned out to be quite an operation. They retired to the living room with cups of tea and sat on the couches. Nick got an easel with a whiteboard and set it up in front of the television. Greg placed a small sand timer on the coffee table. Amber made a scoresheet and set it next to the timer.

"So," Zach said, "this is how we play the Wong version of Pictionary, since Jo and Lily are new to this and Tasha hasn't done it in a while. We'll be in five teams of two tonight. Amber will use a Pictionary word generator and show the word to a member of the first team. They will start drawing, and the other member will have one minute to guess the word. If they do, they get a point, then it moves to the next team. We'll play eight rounds, and then the top two teams make it to the playoffs."

"We're the team to beat," Stuart said, putting his arm around his wife.

"It's true," Zach said to Jo. "My grandparents are terrible at this game, but my parents are freakishly good. I'm sure we can do just as well, though."

They picked Scrabble letters to decide which team would go first. She and Zach got an "A."

"Do you want to draw, or should I?" he asked.

They were sitting on one side of the couch, his leg against hers; Tasha and Greg were sitting at the other end.

"Um, I'll draw." Jo stepped up to Amber, who, as the official judge, was sitting on the chair by the whiteboard. Amber pulled up a word generator on her phone and clicked "generate."

Jo's word was "hipster."

She'd expected something a bit easier, but she could do this. She started drawing a man.

"Man," Zach said.

She added a collared shirt with a checkered pattern.

"Lumberjack."

She added a toque.

"Canadian," he guessed.

Finally, she added glasses and a beard.

"Douche canoe?"

She couldn't help smiling, but dammit, he still wasn't getting this? She'd have to add something to show the hipster's interests.

She drew a bottle of beer.

"Drunk," Zach said.

Unfortunately, it was hard to emphasize that it was craft beer, since presumably writing anything on the bottle would be against the rules.

Next, Jo drew a vinyl record and musical notes, then turned to Zach.

"Um. Musician?"

As his gaze caught hers and she gestured for him to keep guessing, it felt like there was a connection zinging between them.

"Time—"

"Hipster!" Zach said, as the last of the sand in the timer fell.

"Hmph," Ah Ma said. "Not fair, he guessed when the time was up."

"No, it was *almost* up," Zach said. "I got it at the last second."

"I'm the judge, and I say it's fair." Amber drew a single line on the scoresheet. "Point for Team Hipster."

Jo returned to the couch, and Zach settled his arm around her. "Our team names are based on the first thing we draw," he said. "Good job."

He kissed her cheek, and she smiled.

She was determined to get as many points—and kisses—as possible tonight.

Game on.

Stuart and Rosemary were next. Rosemary looked at Amber's phone, then drew the symbol for "male" and a bunch of stick figures below it. All had top hats and angry faces.

Below this, there was a person—a woman?—with long hair and a frown on her face.

Jo had no idea what this word could be.

"Patriarchy," Stuart said.

Rosemary pointed at him and smiled.

How the hell had he gotten patriarchy from that?

Next it was Greg and Tasha's turn. Greg drew first. Whereas everyone else had drawn quick, simple pictures, Greg's was more detailed. It looked like a root vegetable, but which one?

"Carrot," Tasha guessed. "Parsnip. Celeriac. Turnip. Rutabaga. Radish...I'm running out of guesses."

"Time's up," Amber said.

Greg turned away from the whiteboard. "It's obviously wasabi."

"How should I know what that looks like?" Tasha asked. "Why didn't you draw sushi?"

"Then you would have guessed 'sushi.'"

"You could have drawn a little dish with wasabi paste and pickled ginger next to it."

They kept arguing, but when Greg returned to the sofa, Tasha laughed and planted a kiss on his lips, and Jo couldn't help feeling a burst of longing.

Ah Ma and Ah Yeh were up. Ah Ma went to the front and started drawing. Jo tilted her head this way and that, but she had no idea what it was. Next to her, Zach chuckled softly, and it rumbled through her body.

"Garbage can," Ah Yeh said. "Vase. Mug. Teapot. Teacup. Soccer ball."

Ah Ma scrunched up her face in frustration and kept drawing.

"Time's up," Amber said.

"Aiyah, why couldn't you get it?" Ah Ma said. "It was clearly a hot air balloon."

Jo tilted her head again and squinted...and okay, maybe it looked like a hot air balloon, if she really used her imagination.

After the first round, three teams had a point, and two teams did not.

It was Jo and Zach's turn again. When Zach got up from the couch, Jo missed his body heat. He looked at the word on Amber's phone and nodded seriously.

First he drew a rainbow, then an arrow pointing to one of the bands of color.

Ah, he was trying to tell her a color. Clever.

It was the fifth color in the rainbow.

"Blue!" she said.

A ball of joy formed in her chest, though they were just playing Pictionary with his family. But she didn't push the feeling aside. She'd enjoy this night of pretending they were a couple. Of pretending she had what she wanted.

Next, Zach started drawing an odd pattern of swirls. She shook her head, having no idea what that was. Beside it, he drew a finger.

"Blue finger?" she guessed. What on earth could it be? "Blue...fingerprint? Blueprint!"

She laughed when Zach held his hands up in victory.

He sat back down and wrapped his arm around her. She felt gooey, like the filling of a butter tart, and content.

"Mom and Dad, it's your turn," Amber said.

Stuart stepped up to the whiteboard and glanced at his word. When Amber flipped over the timer, he drew an odd shape with a circle in the middle...was that an avocado? Next to it, there was a plus sign, followed by a slice of bread.

"Avocado toast," Rosemary said. "Millennial."

Stuart gave her a thumbs-up.

"I do not understand this one at all," Ah Ma said.

"Two points for both Team Patriarchy and Team Hipster," Amber said.

"Unfair that we have to be Team Patriarchy," Rosemary muttered.

"Well, we can hardly call you Team Millennial. That would be misleading, since you're many decades too old for that."

Rosemary sniffed. "We're not *that* old."

"You could be Team Avocado Toast," Jo suggested.

"I like that," Stuart said.

Jo felt stupidly pleased for getting Zach's father's approval.

But she still wanted to beat him at Pictionary. For some reason, she felt like winning this game, against a happy couple who had been married for almost forty years, would mean something.

Would mean that she and Zach belonged together.

It was foolish, but this was more than just a game to her.

·♥·♥·♥·♥·♥·

An hour later, it was time for the Pictionary finals.

Team Hipster vs. Team Avocado Toast.

Team Lawn Mower—Nick and Lily—had finished third, Team Wasabi in fourth place, and Team Hot Air Balloon in last place.

"Aiyah," Ah Ma said. "This happens every year. We never make the finals."

Zach's grandparents had had a hilariously poor showing, but despite their digs at one another, they seemed to be having a good time.

Jo was gearing herself up for the playoffs, but it wouldn't be easy. She wasn't sure she and Zach could win against a team that had gotten "society" in fifteen seconds.

Seriously. Fifteen seconds!

Jo and Zach were first. Jo drew, and Zach easily guessed "lyrics." Team Avocado Toast wasn't to be outdone, however, and got a point for "extra virgin olive oil."

Zach went up to the whiteboard next. After looking at Amber's phone, he began drawing.

"Airplane," Jo said. It was clearly an airplane, though she doubted that was the word—it would be too easy. "Travel. Vacation. Trip."

Beside the airplane, Zach drew a stick figure lying in a bed, the sun shining above them, a suitcase on the floor beside them.

"Jet lag?"

This correct answer earned Jo a gorgeous smile.

Team Avocado Toast was up. Rosemary guessed "standing ovation" from Stuart's drawing in less than thirty seconds.

"How many rounds are in the playoffs?" Lily asked.

"Four," Amber said. "If there's a tie, we go to sudden death."

Now it was Jo's turn to draw. Her heart was beating extra fast, even though it was only a game of Pictionary.

Her word—or words, rather—was "time zone."

She drew a rough map of Canada and glanced at Zach. He was looking at the whiteboard in puzzlement.

Hmm. Maybe it was a very crude map, but she wasn't accustomed to having to draw their country from memory.

Jo wasn't sure what the time zones did in the territories, but she drew thick lines for the approximate time zone boundaries in the provinces, followed by a clock at three o'clock over BC, a clock showing four o'clock over Alberta, and a clock showing five o'clock over Saskatchewan and Manitoba.

Come on, Zach. You can get this.

"Cross-country," he guessed. "Time. Clocks."

She drew a clock at six o'clock over Ontario, then circled most of Ontario and Quebec.

"Eastern Standard Time?"

She drew another circle around the Central Time Zone—at least, her best guess at where it was. Was she making a mess of this?

"And that's..." Amber began.

"Time zone!" Zach said.

"You got it!" Jo grinned and returned to the couch. "Good job, you."

"No, it was thanks to your wonderful drawing skills."

Jo said nothing, just gestured to the whiteboard, containing her horrible map of Canada. It looked even worse from a distance. Still, he gave her a quick kiss on the temple.

Team Avocado Toast successfully guessed "cheater," and now it was time for the final playoff round. Zach's turn to draw. He frowned when he looked at the word on Amber's phone.

Shit. This was probably a hard one.

Zach drew a wide cylinder, the circular faces horizontal, with a wavy line through the middle—was that supposed to be water? Next, he put a stick figure in the cylinder.

"Tub," Jo said. "Bathtub. Hot tub."

Zach drew another tub of water to the left, except there was no stick figure, and the water line was a little lower. He drew an arrow between the water line in the two tubs. To emphasize that it had moved, perhaps?

Jo wasn't sure what he was getting at, and dammit, she really wanted to win.

Think, Jo. Think.

But she had nothing.

She stared at Zach and willed him to telepathically tell her the word. After all, she was convinced that was how Stuart and Rosemary had gotten some of their words so quickly.

Unfortunately, she got distracted by Zach's forearms. He'd pulled off his sweater and was now wearing just a T-shirt.

Focus.

Zach drew a speech bubble for the stick figure in the tub. Of course, he couldn't actually write any words in it.

Jo looked at the picture again. The water level had increased when the stick figure stepped into the tub. That was displacement. Discovered by Archimedes, right? She remembered learning that in high school science—Zach probably taught it to his students. And when Archimedes had stepped into his tub and suddenly understood displacement, he'd said...

Zach circled the speech bubble.

"Eureka!" Jo shouted.

"Yes!" Zach ran to the couch and lifted her up, and once again, she found herself admiring his arms.

He gave her a peck on the mouth, and now she was admiring his lips.

It had seemed instinctive for him to rush over and kiss her. She couldn't help the way that it warmed her heart.

"You were amazing," he whispered, and that sent tingles through her body.

Rather than sitting next to her on the couch, he pulled her into his lap.

"Get a room," Amber muttered.

Was Jo seducing Zach with her Pictionary skills?

If she'd known this would work so well, she'd have done it ages ago.

Team Hipster had managed to get all four words in the playoffs, but Team Avocado Toast still had a chance to tie.

Indeed, they successfully got "climate."

"I think this is only the second time in Pictionary history that we've needed the sudden death round," Nick said.

Ah Ma patted Jo's knee. "You are so good at this game."

Jo smiled, then walked up to the whiteboard on wobbly legs.

They needed to get this. Somehow, she felt like everything depended on it.

Unfortunately, her word was "shaft."

Shit. The first thing that popped into her head was, unfortunately, not something she wanted to draw in front of Zach's family.

"And...go," Amber said.

Jo stood there for a moment, unsure what to do, before she started drawing a mine shaft.

"Tower?" Zach guessed once she had finished.

She shook her head.

Dammit, this wasn't working. She drew a big "X" through her mine shaft and attempted to draw a shaft of light coming through a window.

"Window," he said. "Sunlight. Morning."

She looked at the time. They were past the halfway point. She needed a new plan.

She *really* wanted to win, and her best chance was to draw a penis in front of Zach's family.

Did she dare?

Chapter 7

ZACH WATCHED AS Jo quickly erased everything she'd drawn.

He had zero idea what this word could be, but he was thrilled that he and Jo were close to defeating his parents. He and Amber had never beaten their parents in the playoffs. Nick and Greg had, but only once, and Zach suspected Mom and Dad had let them win.

Jo, bless her, was the perfect partner who'd gotten more into this game than he'd expected. He'd rarely seen her so animated. It warmed his heart that she fit in with his family.

But it doesn't matter. It's not real.

He pushed aside his momentary disappointment and focused on the whiteboard.

Jo drew a long object with two circles at the base of it. She added some wiggly lines on the balls.

Because...those sure looked like balls, didn't they?

"Cactus," he said, though that made no sense. That was an easy word, and she would have drawn a sensible cactus from the beginning. "Rocket?"

Then Jo drew the head of the penis.

There was no doubt now about what she was drawing.

Everyone else was snickering, but not Zach.

"Penis," he said. "Cock. Balls. Circumcision. Erection."

He couldn't believe he was doing this in front of his parents and grandparents, but he was determined to win this thing.

Jo drew a circle around the center of the drawing, then turned to look at him. Her cheeks were slightly pink, her eyes wide and imploring.

"Shaft!" he exclaimed.

"Yes!" shouted Jo, pointing at him.

"Just in time," Amber said. "I can't believe you went there, Jo."

"Yeah, neither can I."

There was some uncomfortable laughter.

Ah Ma sniffed. "I thought Pictionary was a G-rated game. This is not G-rated."

"The picture isn't quite anatomically correct," Greg said. "For example—"

"I think it's a perfectly good shaft," Zach said.

"Alright," Amber said. "Time to move on. Mom and Dad, if you get this, we'll have to do another round of sudden death overtime. If not, Team Hipster wins."

When Jo came to sit on Zach's lap, he was very aware of a certain part of his anatomy, especially when she wiggled to adjust her position.

Did she know what she was doing to him? Was she wondering if he had a perfectly good shaft?

He couldn't help it; he rather hoped she was.

Amber turned over the timer, and Mom started drawing. There was a man with a beard and a hat. Santa Claus? And now he was drinking a beer?

Zach had no idea what this was, but he wouldn't be surprised if his father still guessed correctly.

Next, Mom drew faces of people laughing.

"Humor? Laughter? Comedy act?" Dad said. "Christmas gone wrong? Drunk Santa?"

Zach stared at the timer and tightened his hold on Jo.

He wanted to defeat his parents, but if he was honest with himself, this was mostly about Jo. About the way she would smile when they won. She was so sexy when she was flushed and excited.

"And..."

"Boxing Day?" Dad said.

"...that's time," Amber said. "Team Hipster wins!"

Jo grinned as though she'd never been happier.

"What was the word?" Dad asked.

"It was 'parody,'" Mom said. "Sorry, I had no idea what to draw. It's hard to show 'parody' when you can't use any words."

"That's okay," Dad said.

Zach wasn't looking at him, though.

He couldn't take his gaze off Jo.

They left at ten o'clock. Zach offered to walk Jo home, like he always did after they went to the bar on Friday nights. But this time, as they made their way across town, there were a couple things different from usual.

First of all, it was slippery.

The temperature had been above freezing for much of the afternoon, and some of the snow had melted, but now the water had turned to ice.

Jo slipped and clung to Zach. To steady her, he wrapped his arm around her body.

The other thing that was different?

He couldn't help wanting to take off her jacket and toque...and more.

They'd made out when they were skating, and he'd replayed their kisses over and over in his head, thinking about what would happen if they went further.

"What was going through your mind," he said, "when you drew a cock and balls on the whiteboard in my parents' living room?"

"Oh, God." She turned away. "I really wanted to win, that's all, and I couldn't think of another way to get you to say 'shaft,' since you didn't get 'mine shaft' or 'shaft of light' from the first two drawings. Your grandma kept giving me dirty looks afterward! I'm mortified."

"Yeah, I figured you just wanted to win."

"I'm sorry."

"It's okay, I like your competitive spirit." He paused. "What else was going through your mind other than winning?"

"Nothing. Nothing at all."

"For example," he pressed, "were you thinking of that particular part of my anatomy?"

"No, your whole family was there!"

The strength of her protest was suspicious, however.

"Mm-hmm," he said. "But my family isn't around now. What are you thinking about?"

"Zach," she said, as though in pain.

"I'll stop right now if you tell me to."

He waited a beat.

She said nothing.

"I think you want to do unspeakably dirty things to my *shaft*," he said quietly.

A strange sound escaped her lips, a mixture of shock and laughter.

No one else was out on the residential street. He stopped walking and pulled her against him, each of his hands holding one of hers.

"May I kiss you again?" he asked.

She nodded quickly and tilted her head upward.

"You're eager," he observed.

"Sorry!" She put a hand over her face.

Jo might have drawn a not-quite-anatomical picture of a penis at his parents' house, but she seemed a touch uncomfortable talking about this stuff. It was cute.

He pulled off his gloves and tucked them into his pocket. Gently, he cupped her cheeks and slipped his fingers under the bottom of her hat.

Then he kissed her, in the quiet of the night, his lips meeting hers over and over. He hadn't thought of doing this with her until recently, but somehow it felt right and *real*, despite the lies they were telling his family.

Jo adjusted herself so that one of her legs was between his, but she lost her balance and knocked into him. He fell backward before he could catch himself, though he managed to land on a snowbank instead of the icy sidewalk.

She fell on top of him, laughing, and kissed him again.

For a moment, neither one of them spoke.

"Jo," he said carefully, "would you want to do this indoors? Maybe on a bed?"

It was the stuff of her fantasies. Jo was walking up the stairs in her house and Zach Wong was following her, his hand resting lightly on her hip.

They were going to her bedroom.

They were going to have sex.

At least, she was pretty sure that's what would happen.

She flicked on the lights in her bedroom and sat on the bed. She should probably strip off her shirt and give him a show, or kiss him against the door, or...something.

But though she could do those things in her imagination, she couldn't do them now.

He sat beside her and pulled her into his lap.

"If you've changed your mind, that's okay," he said.

"No. Not at all. I'm just not very good at initiating stuff. Feeling comfortable with someone new. You know."

Except Zach wasn't "new." She'd known him for ages. They were friends. Maybe that's why she was sharing her inadequacies with him, even though she had a crush on him.

Plus, she'd already drawn a cock in front of his family, so it was hard to feel more embarrassed after that.

"That's one thing I never told you about Matt," she said. "He wished I'd initiate more often. I like sex, but I was always...well. Just a tiny bit awkward about how I look. Not that I think I'm ugly, but my body is more function over form. I can run 10k and play hockey and swim laps, but I hardly look like a model. Anyway, one time, I decided I would try. After dinner, Matt was on the computer, and I told him to join me in the bedroom, with a little wink, you know? I asked him to give me five minutes. I put on sexy underwear and a bra, nothing else, and lay down in bed, waiting for him. After half an hour—"

"*Half an hour?*"

"Yeah. He still hadn't shown up. So I texted him and he didn't reply. He knew how hard this was for me, and he didn't even have the decency to let me know he wasn't interested that night. Then the next week, he asked me again why I didn't initiate."

Zach held her more tightly against him. "That bastard."

He'd called Matt a bastard before, but this time, it was different.

"Anyway," she finished, "that was a few weeks before I ended the engagement. And I haven't been with anyone else since. You're much less out of practice than I am." She shook her head. "Sorry. I'm being weird. I wouldn't blame you if you don't want to do this anymore."

The confused look he gave her was, admittedly, rather gratifying.

"I'm interested, I promise," he said, sliding his hands down to her ass. "Relax and don't worry about anything. I'll take care of you. Just tell me if you ever want to stop, okay?"

"Okay."

He turned on the lamp beside the bed and got up to flick off the main light. It was dim now, the lamp only illuminating part of the room, and it made her feel a little more comfortable somehow.

As he sauntered back to the bed, he pulled his sweater over his head, followed by his T-shirt, exposing his chest. She swallowed as she took in the light and shadows playing over the canvas of his body.

It was nothing she hadn't seen before. She'd seen him in a swimsuit more than once. But this time, he was going to bed with her.

At the back of her mind, she wondered if maybe this wasn't a good idea. He might be physically attracted to her, but he'd never given any indication that he wanted this fake relationship to be not-so-fake, that he harbored anything other than friendly feelings toward her. As far as she knew, he still had no interest in a relationship.

But Jo was suddenly tired of only doing things that were good ideas. The man she craved wanted to be with her tonight, and she wouldn't pass up the opportunity.

"Second thoughts?" he asked. "Want me to cover up?"

"No, that's a terrible idea."

He chuckled as he eased himself on top of her, his chest vibrating against hers. His cock was right *there* between her legs, and he was getting hard. He circled his hips against her, nice and slow, and she groaned. God, that felt nice. When he grasped the bottom of her shirt, she lifted her arms up so he could pull it off, and then he unclasped her bra and tossed it to the side.

She felt a moment of panic that he'd change his mind now, but he didn't.

Instead, he looked at her in awe.

She swallowed past the lump in her throat. She could trust him. He would never make her feel like Matt had.

He started kissing her everywhere. All over her chest, her breasts, her stomach...as though every inch of her was important and deserved attention. She squirmed against him when he pulled her nipple into his mouth and swirled his tongue over the peak. Then he made his way down, and when he got to the waistband of her jeans, he lifted his gaze, and she nodded.

And then he was sliding off her jeans.

Zach was taking off her jeans.

She was nervous, but also excited, and his kisses had helped her relax into the mattress.

He grinned wolfishly when she was wearing just her panties, a pair that was black with a little bow on the front. He slipped his hands under her ass and rolled her over, then pressed his chest against her back. His erection was nestled against her ass, and she moaned as he swept her hair back and kissed her neck before planting a few kisses on her lace-clad ass.

"You're amazing," he whispered, and she smiled into the pillow.

He shucked off his jeans and boxers in one smooth move, and *that* was a sight she'd never seen before.

"What do you think?" He lay down next to her and pumped himself a few times. "Is it a perfectly good shaft?"

She couldn't help the burst of laughter that escaped her lips.

"I don't know," she heard herself say. "I need to touch it first."

Oh my God. Where had *that* come from? It wasn't like her at all.

Zach laughed, his eyes darkening at the same time. He took her hand and brought it down to his crotch.

She very much approved. His cock was hard and filled her hand just right.

She didn't say that, though.

"I still can't tell," she said. "I think I need to put my mouth on it before I can make my final assessment."

He growled low in his throat, and she felt a surge of power.

She was doing this to him.

"Jo..." he said, as he rolled onto his back. "I won't last long."

"I won't take long, then. Just a little lick..." She licked up the underside of his cock and couldn't help squirming as she did so. "And another..." She licked over the head. "And now I'll take the whole thing into my mouth." Her voice shook. "Can't make a proper assessment without doing that, can I?"

He made some inarticulate noises.

She smiled.

Then she took his cock into her mouth and sucked, and he gripped the sheets in his fists.

She released him with a *pop*.

"My expert opinion," she said, "is that it is indeed a perfectly good shaft."

"Just 'perfectly good'?"

"Well, it's quite excellent—does that sound better?"

"I know what would be better." He held her gaze as he pulled off her underwear and tossed them aside. Slowly, he slipped his hand between her legs, and she tensed in anticipation. He slid one long finger inside her and moved it in and out. "God, you're wet."

He still sounded like he was in awe of her.

"For you," she whispered. "Of course I am."

I've wanted you for so long.

He added a second finger, and she could hear her moisture as he moved inside her body. He brought his hand up to his mouth and licked off the first finger, then the second, then his thumb. When he moved his hand back between her legs, he circled his thumb over her clit.

She needed to touch him, too. She reached between his legs and wrapped her hand around his *quite excellent* cock.

"You feel wonderful," he whispered.

Jo had been anxious at first, a little self-conscious, but not anymore.

She ground against his hand. "I need you."

Though he wouldn't know everything that was behind those words, he could give her what she needed at this moment: to feel him within her.

He reached into the pocket of his discarded jeans and pulled out a condom. Her heart raced as she watched him roll it on.

This was really happening.

He held himself above her, and she could barely breathe. He wasn't even inside her yet, and it was already so intense.

The way he looked at her. The way it was easy to be naked with him.

She grasped his erection and positioned it at her entrance. He pushed inside, groaning as he filled her.

Yes. Yes. Yes.

"Zach," she breathed.

He was still for a moment, as though this was almost too much for him, too, and then he started to move, pumping in and out.

He would take care of her. He would give her exactly what she needed. She trusted him.

She hooked her ankles over the backs of his thighs, opening herself up even more, allowing him to go deeper.

"Yes, darling," he said.

He kissed her neck, and she arched up against him as he sucked on her skin. He was hitting every perfect spot inside her; she didn't know how else to explain it, but it was like no sex she'd ever had before.

Her imagination hadn't been up to the task of imagining how good it would feel to be with Zach—which was surprising, because she'd spent a *lot* of time imagining it.

When he raised his body off her, she put her hands on her breasts, pushing them up and tweaking her nipples. He tugged the tip with his teeth before he took as much into his mouth as he could.

She bucked against him, on the precipice, so, so close. If only he could...

He touched his finger to her clit, and she shattered almost immediately, shaking mindlessly and crying out his name, losing herself in her climax.

As she came back down, he gentled his thrusts and looked her in the eyes as though she had just done the greatest thing he'd ever seen.

Eventually, his thrusts became deeper, more powerful, and she felt like he was filling every inch of her, out to her toes and fingertips.

"Jo!" he said as his own climax overtook him.

Half an hour later, they were still lazing in bed, recovering. Neither of them had put on any clothes. Jo enjoyed being naked with Zach. Even if he no longer looked like he wanted to devour her, his eyes continued to roam over her, full of appreciation.

Plus, if she put clothes on, he might feel the need to get dressed, too.

And that would be a calamity.

She gathered up her courage. "Will you stay the night?"

"Of course."

She didn't know what would happen tomorrow, but she wouldn't let herself think about that. For now, she would just enjoy going to sleep next to a man with a perfectly amazing shaft.

Chapter 8

As Zach drifted into consciousness, he became aware of a warm body pressing against his chest. The warm, *naked* body felt wonderful next to his, and he tightened his arms around her.

Yes, he'd woken up snuggling Jo MacGregor.

He felt a moment of panic but told himself to take deep breaths and calm down. Though Zach wasn't usually one to freak out, this was a most unexpected situation, even if he'd been thinking about sleeping with Jo since last week's skating expedition.

Then last night, she'd come over to his parents' house for Chinese New Year. They'd won Pictionary, and she'd horrified his grandmother by drawing a large cock on the whiteboard.

He couldn't help chuckling at the memory.

Then after...

Well.

And now he was snuggling Jo and feeling like all was right in the world, which disturbed him. He'd wanted a fake relationship precisely because he had no interest in a real one.

What was going on?

"Morning." Jo rolled over to face him. There was a bit of makeup smudged under her eyes, and her hair was a mess.

She was just right.

But Chinese New Year was over, and she didn't need to pretend to be his girlfriend anymore.

He couldn't bear the thought, though he didn't care to examine his feelings too closely.

"We never talked about the end of our so-called relationship, did we?" he said casually.

"No, we didn't."

"Wouldn't it be a little suspicious if we broke up right after my family's New Year dinner? They might catch on. Perhaps we should keep doing this for another week or two."

"I think that's an excellent plan."

"You sure you don't mind?"

"I'm quite sure."

She slid her hand down his chest and grasped his erection.

Jo was so much fun in bed. Playful and sexy and eager... He wanted to punch Matt the Douche Canoe for making her feel unwanted and uncomfortable with her sexuality.

But she'd blossomed under Zach's touch last night, responding to everything he did.

He couldn't help feeling a little proud of the way she'd come apart in his arms, and the dopey expression she was giving him now as she leisurely stroked him.

He wanted to touch her, too. In fact, he very much wanted to do something he hadn't had a chance to do last night.

"How about we start the morning off right," he said, "with you sitting on my face?"

She grinned, slow and sexy, and his balls tightened.

Yes, this would be a great morning indeed.

"Hey," Jo said.

"Morning." Tiffany sat down across from her. "What's so important that you need a Sunday morning tea-and-scone date at the bakery?"

Jo leaned forward and lowered her voice. "I slept with Zach last night!"

"And it was good?"

"Do I look like I had bad sex?"

Tiffany regarded her for a moment. "Nah, you look like you had amazing sex. I bet everyone in here can tell."

"Tiff!"

"Just kidding."

Jo glared at her friend, then went back to thinking about last night. "It really was amazing," she said dreamily. "He was so sweet and attentive, and he made me feel like I *mattered*, more than Matt ever did. And this morning, he said he'd like to extend our fake relationship a little longer. I said yes, of course, but I wish he wanted a real relationship, and he didn't say anything about that."

"He might just want to get laid again."

"Yeah, maybe he wants to use me for sex." *Using someone* didn't seem like Zach, though. "Or maybe he's trying to figure things out. Maybe he's developing feelings for me."

Tiffany looked at her sadly.

The excitement Jo had felt over having great sex with the man she loved started to fade. Perhaps it was delusional to think he was starting to develop feelings, and if she just waited, it would happen.

It was risky, too. After the intimacy she'd shared with Zach, she could already feel herself getting more attached. Her sky-high fantasies about the sex hadn't been dashed by the real thing, and they'd woken up cuddling, for God's sake.

Jo sighed. She'd allow herself to continue this fake relationship...for now. Zach was right—it would be odd if they broke up right after she met his family.

·♥ · ♥ · ♥ · ♥ · ♥ ·

Sometimes when Zach's brothers were in Mosquito Bay for the weekend, he'd invite them over to knock back a beer or two. This Sunday afternoon was one of those days. However, Zach was now regretting his decision.

"I can't believe your girlfriend drew a giant dick in front of Ah Ma and Ah Yeh!" Nick slapped his knee and laughed. They were all sitting on the couches in the living room. "It must have been...what would you say, Greg? Was the dick twelve inches, or longer?"

Greg grunted in response, but the corners of his lips tilted up.

Zach wasn't used to being in a bad mood, but he'd been like this since Jo left this morning. "Thanks, Mr. Fancypants," he said to Nick.

Nick took a sip of his beer. "So you and Jo, eh? How long has this been going on?"

"Two weeks."

"Did something bad happen? You're even grumpier than Greg."

"Thank you," Greg said.

"I'm fine," Zach said in a clipped voice.

Nick drummed his fingers on the table. "I thought you swore off dating after Marianne left you."

"Well, you didn't date either until you met Lily."

"Guess I was waiting for the right woman. Is Jo the right woman? Is she your true wuv?"

Nick was teasing Zach the way Zach had teased Nick about Lily.

Yeah, on some level, Zach felt like he deserved this.

However, he wanted to set the record straight. Just with his brothers.

"Jo isn't my girlfriend," he said. "I just asked her to pose as my girlfriend for Chinese New Year so nobody would try to set me up with another woman. I didn't need a repeat of Thanksgiving, thank you very much. Don't tell anyone, okay?"

Nick scratched his head. "But you two have been dating for a couple weeks."

"Had to make our relationship believable."

"You were sure doing a good job of being affectionate."

Zach shrugged. "I'm a good actor, what can I say?"

"No, I think you're secretly in love with her, and now that Chinese New Year is over, you're mourning the loss of your fake relationship." Nick laughed. "Can't believe you got a fake girlfriend!"

"The possibility actually occurred to me yesterday morning," Greg said. "But then I brushed it aside as too ridiculous. Guess I was wrong."

"It's not over yet," Zach said. "I asked her to extend the act a little longer. It would be suspicious if we broke up immediately after Chinese New Year, right?"

"Aww." Nick put his hands over his heart. "You really do love her."

"No, I don't."

Why was he telling his brothers about this?

Well, he could use some advice, he supposed, though whether he could get anything useful out of Nick and Greg was questionable.

He took a deep breath. "We slept together last night."

Nick grinned. "Ah. She wanted to see if your shaft looked like her drawing."

"I sure hope it doesn't," Greg said. "Or your dick isn't normal."

"Alright," Zach said. "Enough. No more talk about the Pictionary game, okay?"

Nick leaned forward and rested his arms on his knees. "So you slept together. Was it bad? Is that why you're in a crappy mood?"

"It was not *bad*," Zach said.

"Ah," Greg said sagely, nodding his head. "It was the best you've ever had, and that disturbed you."

Zach said nothing.

Unfortunately, his brothers read a lot into that.

"You love her," Nick said. "I was right."

"I don't love her," Zach protested, "but I do want to do it again. I've had a bit of a dry spell lately—that must be the reason."

"It could be. Or maybe you're meant to be together. Personally, I vote for the latter."

Geez, Nick had gotten annoying since he'd started seeing Lily.

"You asked her to continue your fake relationship," Nick said. "I think you're in denial. Next thing you know, you'll be making her soup dumplings and butter tarts and ordering your family to make you a snow fort."

"Hey." Greg crossed his arms over his chest. "I didn't *order* you. You helped willingly."

"Yeah, we were willing to help," Zach said. Greg and Tasha, his high school girlfriend, had always seemed like they belonged together. "But your control-freak side really came out when we were helping you with that snow fort."

"Agreed," Nick said. "You were a pain-in-the-ass."

Greg grunted.

"Back to your problem." Nick turned to Zach. "I still think you're in love with Jo, but you can't accept it yet. And I feel your pain. I've been there before. But you don't need to be so frightened."

"I'm not frightened." Zach was just being logical after the implosion of his engagement.

Greg gave him a not-so-comforting slap on the shoulder.

"I like Jo," Nick said. "She's nice, and she's not afraid to draw pictures of giant dicks in front of your family. Always a winning combination."

God, Zach would hear about that dick pic for years to come.

Although, admittedly, the memory did make his lips twitch. The look on Ah Ma's face had been priceless.

His brothers had been of no assistance today, but that was okay. Zach was sure these weird feelings would disappear soon.

He couldn't help hoping that he and Jo would sleep together a couple more times, though. Another week or two of casual sex between friends, and then she'd be out of his system, right?

Chapter 9

On Wednesday, Zach was marking chemistry exams, but it wasn't going well.

He kept thinking about a different kind of chemistry.

He texted Jo. *Want to come over after dinner?*

She didn't immediately respond. He kept checking his phone every minute, feeling pathetic. She was busy at work, of course. She had an important job. Perfectly reasonable for her not to respond right away.

But to sweeten the offer, he added, *Actually, you can come over for dinner. I'll cook.*

At lunch, she replied, *Sounds good!*

He didn't pump his fist in the air. No, he most certainly did not.

That evening, after much debate, he made chicken alfredo and Caesar salad, cursing himself for not having gotten the ginger beef recipe yet. He also bought one of the currant scones she liked from the bakery.

As they ate dinner, they talked about their days at work, including Jo's attempts to expand her repertoire of balloon animals. It all seemed horribly domestic, but he reminded himself that they were simply friends having dinner together. Nothing weird about that, right?

And afterward...

It turned out to be a very good night.

However, it hadn't gotten her out of his system. But surely another couple times and he'd be happy to go back to being friends, not friends with benefits in a fake relationship.

On Friday, they met at Finn's as usual, but their regular table was taken by some out-of-towners, so they sat at the bar.

He shifted his bar stool close to hers, so his hip pressed against her, and placed his hand on her leg. She looked up at him from beneath her long eyelashes, and God, he wanted her.

Okay, maybe it would take more than a couple times.

This wasn't love, though. Love might not happen instantly, but there was always a spark from the beginning. He'd been in love four times—he knew this. Plus, that's how it had been for Nick and Lily. Greg and Tasha—that was a little different, as they'd known each other for most of their lives.

But he and Jo had known each other for a long time, too.

Except, not really.

He'd known *of* her, but three years was a huge age difference when you were a kid. They hadn't become friends until they'd both ended up here, at Finn's, disappointed by the people they were supposed to marry. They'd been friends for four years now, and okay, he was suddenly attracted to her, but that didn't mean he was falling in love.

It just meant he hadn't had much sex in the past year, and Jo was here, and convenient, and very lovely.

How had he never noticed that before?

As she sipped her Guinness, he watched her throat, which he'd kissed on Wednesday night. She always drank Guinness at the bar. He wasn't a fan, but it was her favorite beer, and now he found that rather charming, like the way she'd slide her hand up her neck and smile shyly at him.

He needed to get them back to their simple friendship.

"You excited for the hockey game on Sunday?" he asked.

"Yeah, we're going to kick their ass," she said, her competitive spirit coming out. "Can't believe we lost last year."

Every year on Groundhog Day, there was a hockey game between Mosquito Bay and the nearest town to the north, Ashton Corners. They charged admission and sold snacks, and the proceeds went to charity. Last year, Mosquito Bay had lost for the first time in five years, and Jo hadn't been happy. She was usually fairly easygoing, but when she really got into something...

"We'll win this time." He didn't care about the outcome much, but he wanted Jo to have what she wanted.

Just because he was her friend, that was all.

Both towns' teams were mostly male, but Jo was one of two women on their team. Suddenly, the thought of her whipping down the ice on a breakaway turned him on.

What the hell?

He wouldn't let himself get too worked up about it. It was just because they were sleeping together. It didn't mean anything.

Alright. Time to return to what had started their friendship: their break-ups. That was a safe topic, and it would remind him of why he never wanted another serious relationship.

"Did you always plan to return to Mosquito Bay after dental school?" he asked. This wasn't directly about his break-up, but thinking about staying or leaving Mosquito Bay made him think of Marianne, as Jo would know.

"I did go off to university with the intention of going to dental school after undergrad. My dad talked about me taking over his practice, and at first, I didn't like the idea. I was determined to do everything all by myself, start over on the other side of the country, or at least on the other side of the province." She chuckled, then said with a shrug, "I was a teenager. But after a few years of living in Hamilton, I tired of city life. My dad was getting old, and I knew how much it would mean to him if I came back to Mosquito Bay. By the time I got into dentistry, that was my goal. A stable job, my family nearby. A quiet life, but I like it."

"Me, too." *I like that you came back here. I like that you're a part of my life.*

He took a gulp of beer and looked at the television above the bar. There was a game on, but he hadn't paid any attention to it until now because he'd been talking to Jo.

"I looked forward to going away for school," he said, "although I didn't spend much time thinking about what I'd do with my life afterward. But a part of me always thought I'd come back, if I was able to get a job in the area, even though..."

"What is it?"

He turned toward her. "My family isn't like most of the other families in Mosquito Bay. There's the Chin-Williams, but they've all left now, and the Lee family that runs the convenience store. The Lams are good friends of my parents, but they live in Ashton Corners. We don't quite fit in. Nick was always very aware of that, and he hated it. For me, it wasn't a big deal—maybe it helps that my appearance doesn't make me stand out as much. Either way, this is my home, and it's not perfect, but I like it. Marianne thought she'd like it, too."

As long as we're together, it doesn't matter where we are, Marianne had said. Zach had been a stupid young man, and he'd believed her. Besides, it wasn't like she'd come from Toronto; she'd grown up in a small city. And Mosquito Bay wasn't isolated, unlike some of the towns up north. Inland from Mosquito Bay, it was farming country, and there were towns every ten or fifteen kilometers. London and Sarnia weren't all that far. Toronto was less than three hours away.

It hadn't been enough, though.

But all his bitterness was gone now. The thought of Marianne didn't cause the pain in his heart that it once had. In fact, he realized this wasn't anything new; he hadn't thought of her much in the last year or two.

Jo nodded and squeezed his hand.

Jo, whose plans for life weren't incompatible with his. She'd grown up here, too, and she'd lived here as an adult for several years. He didn't see her changing her mind about this. Jo was pretty steady, and she knew what she wanted.

And one of the things she wanted was another relationship.

As long as she kept sleeping with him, she couldn't have a boyfriend—unless she was into such arrangements, but he didn't think she was.

Just a little longer. Surely it wouldn't take much longer, and then he'd let her go. He'd encourage her to date and pursue what she wanted.

But for tonight...

He placed his hand on her leg, his fingers gently stroking her inner thigh.

Jo made an inarticulate noise that sounding like "gunhhh."

"Any plans tomorrow?" he asked conversationally, as though he wasn't touching her.

"Some...cleaning," she managed to say. "And..." She shook her head, then hissed, "What are you doing?"

"Oh, nothing." He circled his thumb over the inside of her knee. It seemed to be a particularly sensitive part.

"Zach..."

She was pretending to be annoyed with him, and it was kind of adorable.

But truth be told, he couldn't keep this up much longer.

"Want to get out of here?" he asked.

This time, they went to his house. He recalled how tentative she'd been last weekend, but there was none of that today. It thrilled Zach that she felt comfortable enough to push him up against the front door and pin his hands at his sides.

Her kisses were wet and sloppy and tinged with Guinness, but he didn't mind. She tasted fantastic. Guinness and *Jo*.

His jeans were getting very tight.

He freed his hands from her grasp and dragged down the zipper on her jacket. She was still kissing him as though her life depended on it, as though nothing was more important than this kiss.

And perhaps nothing was.

He needed to touch her. He bunched up her sweater with one hand, and his other hand unbuttoned her jeans and slid inside her panties. He groaned as he encountered her wetness.

"You're so sexy," he breathed.

"You really think that." It wasn't a question; she was just stating it with wonder in her voice.

"Of course I do." He ran his finger over her slit and released a shuddering breath.

Zach shucked off his coat, got down on his knees, and looked up at her. She was still wearing her jacket—though it was unzipped—and her hat and her boots, but it would take too long to remove them now.

He pushed down her jeans and underwear and put his mouth between her legs.

She gripped his hair, and that wasn't unpleasant, not at all.

He hadn't gotten to do enough of this last weekend, but he'd make up for it now. When he gave her one long lick, she threw her head back against the door. Encouraged, he licked her more urgently and slid two fingers inside her tight channel. She clenched around him, and God, he couldn't stand it anymore. With his other hand, he unzipped his own jeans, removed his cock from the opening in his boxers, and started stroking himself as he pleasured her. When he glanced up, she was looking down at his cock, and then, goddammit, she licked her lips.

"Zach..."

He'd never tire of hearing her utter his name like that.

Jo said his name again as her legs slipped out from under her, her back sliding down the door until her ass came to rest on the floor.

And the whole time, he was pleasuring her.

Her hands were in his hair again, urging him on. He moved his fingers faster, in and out, and stroked his dick more quickly, too.

Jo wasn't a screamer, but she gasped and jerked as her climax overtook her. Her head tipped back, exposing the column of her throat; he looked up at her face as he continued to lick her and help her wring every last bit of pleasure from this.

Afterward, she collapsed on the carpet in the hallway, but she didn't have the blissed-out expression that he'd expected. Instead, her eyes roved over him hungrily.

"Take it off," she said.

He didn't know what she was referring to, so he took off everything. His shirt, his pants, his boxers.

She reached for his cock and pumped it a few times. When he pulled a condom out of his pants, she rolled it on.

And then she sank down on him, right on the carpet near his front door.

Had he ever had sex here before?

He didn't think so.

But his thoughts were wiped from his mind as she began to ride him. He loved seeing her above him, like a brilliant goddess. She leaned forward and pressed her breasts against his chest and kissed his mouth.

Possessiveness curled through him. He bet she wasn't like this with anyone but him.

He cupped her ample ass in his hands and urged her on. He buried his face between her breasts and sucked on one.

When he could take it no more, when he felt the need to be in control, he twisted them over so he was on top.

For a moment, though, he didn't move. He just held himself above her and grinned, and she squirmed beneath him, her pretty brown hair fanned out on the carpet.

"Zach," she said, "fuck me."

Those words, tumbling from her lips...

He pushed into her again and again, each stroke more intense than the last, as she writhed beneath him. When he licked his thumb and pressed it to her clit, her eyes opened wide, and when she pushed up against him one more time, she emitted the prettiest sigh he'd ever heard, and he growled as he found his release inside her.

As he came back down, and they lay there with their arms around each other, just inside the door to his house, he started laughing. He couldn't believe they hadn't been able to wait to get to his bedroom—or at least a couch.

Jo tucked her body closer to his and laughed, too.

He felt a bone-deep satisfaction that he hadn't experienced in a long, long time.

When Zach woke up, he was cold, and it was still dark out.

He checked his alarm clock. It was three in the morning.

The reason he was cold? He was naked and didn't have any blankets. Jo, apparently, was a blanket stealer, which was rather charming, actually. He was pleased to learn this detail about her.

Stealthily, he slid over to her side of the bed. She had a strong grip on the blankets, and he had to tug firmly to get them out of her hands.

"Zach," she murmured.

He wasn't sure whether she was conscious or not.

"Why are you taking my blankets." She sounded a little more awake now, but still vulnerable; he felt special for being able to see her at a moment like this.

Not that he could see anything but shadows in the dark room, but he could touch her and hear her.

"I'm freezing," he said. "You're hogging the blankets."

"Am not."

"Are too."

"Oh. So I am."

She adjusted the blankets so he was covered, then snuggled up against him, her front pressed against his back. He was the little spoon.

He enjoyed having her arms around him. And he had blankets on top of him now, so he was cozy and warm. He could stay here forever, cocooned in the darkness with her. He still felt that deep satisfaction from earlier, like he was exactly where he belonged.

After a while, however, Jo wiggled against him and stroked her hand over his chest, and he started to get hard.

He rolled over and slipped his hand between her legs, finding her slick with moisture.

"Yes," she murmured.

As he slid his finger inside her and she moaned, he realized something terrifying.

There was no way he'd be able to "get her out of his system."

It would never be enough.

Zach had fallen asleep soon after their middle-of-the-night sex, but Jo was still awake.

When she'd felt hopeless about her crush before, she used to console herself with the thought that maybe the sex would be bad.

But that was the exact opposite of the truth.

He made her feel sexy, desired, and completely comfortable to initiate things. Why, she'd pushed him up against the door and stuck her tongue down his throat, and that hadn't been weird, not at all. Nor had it been weird when she'd said, "fuck me."

She'd forgotten it could be like this. Both the sex, as well as the quiet moments cuddling in bed together, when it felt like all was right in the world.

Maybe it had never quite been like this for her before.

She was falling even more in love with him.

But he was still Zach Wong, and he hadn't said anything more about what was going on between them. In fact, tonight he'd asked if she'd always planned to come back to Mosquito Bay after university, and she'd figured he was thinking of Marianne.

It didn't seem like he wanted anything close to what she wanted.

And she deserved better, didn't she?

She'd deserved better than the sex she'd had with Matt; she'd deserved a partner who'd actually respond—even if it was to say he wasn't interested that night—when she put herself out there and tried to initiate.

She deserved the sex she had with Zach.

But she also wanted a relationship, and she shouldn't settle for a guy who seemed to have no intention of giving that to her.

She should stop sleeping with him, but the thought of giving up that intimacy made tears prick at the back of her eyes. She liked being able to show him how she felt even if she couldn't tell him. She liked feeling good about her body.

Just a bit longer...and then maybe she should give up their friendship, too.

She hated the thought. Their friendship had been a great comfort to her after her break-up with Matt, the thing she looked forward to every week, even before her crush.

However, she needed to move on, and as long as she kept seeing Zach at least once a week, it would be hard for her to extricate herself.

She needed a clean break.

Next to her, Zach released a single snore, and she laughed through the tears that were now falling down her cheeks. She wanted more nights like this.

She snuggled up close, careful not to wake him or steal the blankets.

Just a little longer...

Chapter 10

There were twenty seconds left in the game. The score was tied at four.

Zach, who'd assisted on Mosquito Bay's second goal, was on the bench next to Shawn, but Jo was on the ice. His eyes didn't follow the puck. They stayed on her.

And then she got a breakaway and he was yelling.

She was going to do it!

When she was a couple meters from the net, she took her shot...

...and scored.

Of course his Jo didn't miss.

His? Well, they'd been fake dating for a few weeks. He supposed he was used to the idea of being with her.

When the game was over and she skated over to the bench, he took off his helmet and greeted her with a kiss. A few people whistled, but he ignored them.

"You were amazing," he said.

"So were you."

"Not as good as you."

She laughed a little, but he could tell she was proud.

They all went out for beers at Finn's afterward, and he kept close to her side the whole time. He didn't want to leave her, but he could only stay for an hour—he had other plans.

When he got back to his house, Sebastian Lam was already there. Sebastian had been back in Ontario since December, but he'd only contacted Zach last week. And he hadn't gone to the hockey game—hockey wasn't really his thing.

Sebastian and Zach were the same age. They'd attended different elementary schools, since the Lam family lived in Ashton Corners, but they'd seen each other all the time as kids and been best friends. Later, they'd gone to high school together.

It had been a few years since they'd seen each other, though, as Sebastian had gone to med school out west and stayed there to do his residency. He'd returned to be a family physician in a small town near Stratford.

"Good to see you, man," Zach said, giving his friend a back-slapping hug.

"Same," Sebastian said gruffly. He was about the same height as Zach, but a bigger, sturdier guy.

They went inside and Zach pulled out a beer for each of them. They sat at opposite ends of the couch in the living room, and for a minute, it was quiet.

They were good friends who'd hardly seen each other in years. Shouldn't they have something to say?

Zach was miffed that Sebastian hadn't contacted him earlier, that he'd had to hear it from his parents, but he wasn't sure he should bring it up. And the biggest thing happening in his life was his fake relationship with Jo, but he didn't know what he wanted to reveal about that.

Though Zach was usually the chattier of the two, it was Sebastian who broke the silence.

"You're probably wondering why I didn't text you earlier," Sebastian said. "Honestly, I was avoiding you."

Zach wasn't sure how to respond.

"Why?" he finally managed.

"Because I hadn't been back for long when I started...well." Sebastian took a pull on his beer. "Seeing your sister."

"You're seeing Amber?"

"Last I checked, you only had one sister."

"Thanks, smart ass. Are you, like, officially her boyfriend?"

"What is this?" Sebastian grunted. "High school again?"

"You know what I mean."

Are you just sleeping together? Is there any kind of commitment?

Sebastian shrugged.

It seemed Sebastian wasn't quite sure what was going on with Amber, just like Zach wasn't sure what was going on with Jo.

Except that wasn't true, right? They were friends who were sleeping together and faking a relationship. It was simple, really. He knew exactly what was going on.

Then why does it feel like I've been pushed into the deep end?

Zach shook his head to clear his thoughts.

"Okay," he said to Sebastian. "You're seeing my sister. You're less of a bastard than her exes, so...cool. You don't know exactly where you stand, but you'll sort it out, I'm sure. You were worried about telling me this?"

Yes, it was a little weird and it would take time to wrap his mind around it. Especially since Sebastian and Amber were such different people. Amber was...not precisely irresponsible, but free-spirited, and more artsy than the rest of them, despite her poor Pictionary skills. Sebastian was nothing like her.

But Zach was fine with this. Truly.

"I figured you'd be cool about it, but Amber wasn't sure." Sebastian paused. "Thanks."

Zach wanted to pry, but he didn't.

"I hear your parents tried to set you up with my sister at Thanksgiving," Sebastian said, a little smirk on his face.

"Yeah, they did. It was a disaster."

Sebastian's smirk widened. "Can't believe your parents found dates for all of you. And Nick is now dating Greg's date?"

Zach nodded.

"Thank God my parents have never attempted anything like that."

"Do your parents know about you and Amber?" Zach asked, then realized what he was saying. "No, of course they don't, or they would have immediately called up my parents, who would have then knocked on my door."

Sebastian chuckled. "Yup, exactly, which is why I don't want you to tell them."

"Don't worry, I won't."

"I'll figure this out soon, I promise."

Zach wanted to tell Sebastian to treat his sister right and all that fun stuff, but he knew it didn't need to be said. His friend was a good guy.

"What's this I hear about you and Jo MacGregor?" Sebastian asked, clearly having had enough of talking about his own dating life.

"We've been seeing each other for a month." Zach looked down at his beer and tried to hide his goofy smile. *Where did that come from?*

He didn't end up telling Sebastian the truth.

For some reason he liked the idea of Sebastian thinking it was real.

❤ · ❤ · ❤ · ❤ · ❤

"One last Friday, and that's it," Jo said to Tiffany. They were at the bakery, each with a hot chocolate in hand. "You were right. Nothing more is going to happen with Zach. He just doesn't see me that way."

She choked up on the last words. She hated admitting it out loud. Hated that she'd spent so long in love with someone who wouldn't love her back.

And yet, in the middle of the night when he...

She shut down that train of thought. It wasn't going anywhere productive.

She wouldn't regret the last few weeks, though. Wouldn't regret knowing what it was like to go on dates with Zach and kiss him and wake up with him.

But it was time to move on. She'd allow herself one more night, and that was it.

"Oh, Jo," Tiffany said, squeezing her hand. "I hate that I was right. You know that."

Jo blinked back tears and forced herself to laugh instead. "I can't believe I was in a fake relationship. Doesn't it sound ridiculous?"

Before Tiffany could answer, an older woman approached their table.

It was Shelly Sanderson. Shit. Had she heard what Jo said?

If she had, she gave no indication of it.

"Just want to congratulate you on your fabulous goal in the hockey game, dear," she said before bustling off to the front of the bakery.

When Jo arrived at her parents' house that night, Mom, Dad, and Becky looked at her with sad smiles, even though Jo had scored the game-winning goal against Ashton Corners.

They knew. They had to know.

Jo couldn't help but be annoyed with their pitying looks. *Poor Jo, she's already thirty-three and she can't get more than a fake relationship.*

"Shelly Sanderson overheard you and Tiffany at the bakery earlier," Mom said as she steered Jo into the kitchen. "Apparently you weren't really in a relationship with Zach? You were just pretending?"

Jo nodded. She didn't see the point in trying to lie now. "He had reasons for wanting his family to think he had a girlfriend, and I said I'd play along."

"Why didn't you tell us the truth?"

"It wouldn't be a good fake relationship if lots of people knew it wasn't real, would it?"

Ugh. If only Shelly would go back to making her coconut lemon squares and stop gossiping so much.

"You have a good career," Mom said. "And a house and friends and hobbies—"

"I know," Jo snapped, even though she *never* snapped at her mother. "I have a great life. I just want someone to share it with. I won't apologize for wanting more."

She didn't admit she had a crush on Zach, and she certainly didn't admit how intimate their fake relationship had become.

"Maybe you shouldn't have broken things off with Matt, then," Mom said.

"No, I absolutely should have. I regret not ending it earlier. It's not unreasonable to..."

...to want a man who looks at me the way Zach does.

She would end things with him and put this behind her. She would *not* settle for less than she deserved. Maybe it would take her a long time to find the right guy, but that was okay.

"Excuse me for a minute," she said.

She needed a moment to compose herself, and she needed to do one more thing.

Sorry, I can't see you this Friday, she texted Zach. *Something came up.*

Spending one last night with him would be too painful, and she should start the process of moving on as soon as possible.

Shelly Sanderson overheard me telling Tiffany that our relationship was fake, so if your family finds out the truth, I'm sorry about that, too.

She couldn't bring herself to tell him that their friendship was over. Besides, she owed him more than a text. She didn't see how she could face him this week, though; she needed a little more time.

Jo walked out of the washroom with her head held high.

If she could score that great goal, she could handle dinner with her family and a Friday night alone.

Chapter 11

Ouch.

Zach rubbed his cheek, where he'd just been hit with a basketball.

"What's wrong, Mr. Wong?"

"Why aren't you paying attention?"

The senior boys' basketball team came to stand in a group around him. Seven thirty in the morning was too early for this, especially since he hadn't gotten a good night's sleep last night.

In fact, he hadn't had a good night's sleep in a while now, and he constantly found himself reaching for Jo, even though she wasn't there. He wished he would wake up cold, without blankets, because at least that would mean she was in his bed to steal them.

"Lady troubles?" asked one of the boys.

"Apparently he's dating Dr. MacGregor."

"No, they were just pretending, didn't you hear?"

"Enough," Zach said in an unusually stern voice. "I'm going outside for a minute, and when I get back, you guys better be doing drills, not gossiping about my personal life, okay?"

He exited through the doors that led to the parking lot and breathed in the cold air. It was below freezing, and the snow was falling lightly. It reminded him of the day he and Jo had gone to the skating trail up near Goderich.

Goddammit. Today was Friday, and he always looked forward to Friday night. It was his time to hang out with Jo.

Strangely, though, she'd said she had plans today.

She never had plans on Friday night, except with him.

He couldn't help feeling a bit bereft.

He'd been looking forward to seeing her at the bar, and maybe afterward, they'd go back to his place and have sex, then wake up wrapped around each other and do it again. That was what he'd become accustomed to in the past couple weeks.

And the Friday nights at Finn's—he'd been accustomed to those for the past four years.

Fuck, it was cold out here, though it was nice to feel something other than the pain of not seeing her.

He'd slowly been realizing it over the past week or two, but now, it was crystal clear.

He wished their relationship were real.

Zach hadn't thought love could work this way for him, and he'd done his best to protect his heart ever since Marianne left. But it had snuck up on him.

He loved Jo's intelligence and athleticism. Her laugh, her smile. The way she could make people feel at ease. The way she could be strong and vulnerable with him at the same time.

It had never been "just sex" with Jo.

He needed her back in his life. He needed to wake up with her again and again. He needed to watch her draw more phallic objects in front of his family and score more game-winning goals.

Except he didn't want another relationship. He'd sworn them off—and for good reason.

He scrubbed his hand over his face.

Screw it. He was heading out of town tonight.

At nine o'clock that night, Zach was in Toronto with Nick, Lily, Greg, and Tasha. They were sitting around a table at a busy restaurant on King Street, drinking Thai iced tea and eating grabong, a Thai version of deep-fried shredded vegetables. Zach picked up a piece of squash and dipped it in the sauce—he had no idea what was in the sauce, but it was tasty.

"So, what's with the sudden decision to come to Toronto for the weekend?" Nick asked.

"I missed you guys."

His brothers looked at him skeptically.

"You saw us at Chinese New Year," Greg said.

"I know." Zach took a deep breath. "I'm falling for Jo, but I was in denial. You two were right."

"Sounds like it pained you a lot to say that," Nick said. "Hard to admit we're smarter than you, I guess?"

Zach gave him a look. "Yeah. But worse, I swore I'd never fall in love again."

Nick turned to Lily. "He was engaged once, but his fiancée left him."

"She didn't want to live in Mosquito Bay anymore," Zach said.

"I don't blame her," Nick said, "but Jo's made a life in Mosquito Bay. I doubt she has any intention of leaving. It's not the same."

"Still. The idea of having a relationship again, giving someone the power to hurt me that much..." Zach helped himself to more deep-fried squash.

There wasn't any food like this in Mosquito Bay. The only Thai food in town was the recent addition of pad Thai to the menu at Wong's Wok.

But Zach was content to take the occasional trip to the city to enjoy such things. He didn't need them all the time.

He enjoyed visiting Toronto, but he wouldn't want to live here. It was too much, and everyone you passed on the street was a stranger.

"A lot of things that are worth having involve risk," Lily said.

"Very true," Greg agreed.

"What if she doesn't feel the same way?" Zach asked.

"You feel like a fool in front of one person," Nick said. "Are you more scared of telling her and being rejected, or of what could happen if you started a relationship and it doesn't work out later on?"

"The second. But also the first."

"I'm not sure you need to worry about that one," Tasha said. "It was pretty clear at Chinese New Year that she had feelings for you. When Greg told me you guys were faking it, I had a hard time believing it. I bet she's been in love with you for a long time, Zach, and that's why it was so easy for her to act as your girlfriend. And you've been unable to see what was right in front of you until now."

He felt a burst of hope. Had Jo really been in love with him before their fake relationship? For how long? Why had she never said anything?

The answer was obvious. She would have known he'd shoot her down.

They'd started sleeping together, but he'd only said he wanted to extend their fake relationship, and now she was trying to step back before she got hurt more.

His heart clenched. He felt terribly for her.

Or maybe she hadn't been in love with him before, and he just liked Tasha's explanation because it assuaged some of his fears.

But even if Jo returned his feelings, and even though he was pretty sure she wanted the same future as he did, what if they broke up?

"That's no guarantee," he said hoarsely as the waitress set his khao soi in front of him. He took a bite of the crispy noodles on top, then dipped his chopsticks into the broth and stirred the beef and noodles.

"No," Nick said, "but like Lily said, sometimes you have to take risks. Which is something you're not great at doing. You live in your hometown. You work at the high school you attended."

Zach enjoyed his simple life, and he didn't like having to defend his choices. There wasn't somewhere else he'd rather live, another career he'd rather have.

Except now there was another person he wanted.

Jo.

His brothers had a point. His life hadn't made him very good at taking risks, and this felt like a huge risk. His last relationship had failed, and his feelings for Jo were quite strong, if he was honest with himself.

"How do I do it?" he asked.

"Well, you could try Greg's snow fort idea," Nick said, "but you'll just have Mom and Dad to help you, not us."

"That's not what I mean. How do you mentally prepare yourself to do something scary?"

God, he felt like a wuss.

"Roller coasters," Greg said cryptically.

"Roller coasters?"

"You liked them when you were young, even though you'd always freak out a bit when we were in line at the amusement park."

"And horror movies," Nick said.

"I wouldn't compare Jo to a horror movie."

"I just mean," Greg said, "that sometimes scary things are great experiences. You have to remind yourself of that. I know you're afraid of rejection and of it not working out, but won't you regret it even more if you never try?"

That was a good point.

"I'm fucked either way," Zach said, but at the same time, hope fluttered in his chest.

"Basically, yeah," Greg grunted.

But Zach looked at his brothers and their partners—Tasha sneaking a shrimp off Greg's plate, which Greg didn't fail to notice, and Nick resting his hand on

Lily's shoulder—and felt an intense longing to have the same thing with Jo.

Just her. He didn't want a relationship if it was with anyone else.

There was no guarantee, but he'd gotten through heartbreak once before. It had sucked, but he'd done it. He had to try.

After spending the night in Nick's guest room, Zach drove back to Mosquito Bay. Instead of going to his place, he went to his grandparents' house—the one they'd bought five years after arriving from Hong Kong and had lived in for decades—and parked in the driveway.

He knocked on the door, hoping only his grandfather would be home and he could ask a little favor without too much drama.

Alas, after five minutes, he sighed and had to accept the truth.

Nobody was here, which almost certainly meant Ah Yeh and Ah Ma were visiting Zach's parents. So Zach headed to his parents' house.

"We were just talking about you," Mom said when he stepped inside.

"Good things?" Zach inquired.

Ah Ma marched into the front hall and pointed a menacing finger at him. "You lied to us. You were not dating Jo. You were faking it!"

Oh, dear. The gossip had reached his family.

Zach ran his hands through his hair. "It's true."

"Really?" Mom said. "I was convinced Shelly was wrong."

He shook his head. "No, it's true. I asked Jo to pretend to be my girlfriend because I was afraid of the matchmaking you guys would attempt for Chinese New Year, after what happened at Thanksgiving."

"Yes, we did overstep there a little..." Mom admitted.

Ah Ma, however, did not feel the same way. "Don't worry, I will set you up with four women at Easter to make up for it. I am glad you are not with Jo." She clucked her tongue. "I don't approve of her."

Anger coursed through Zach's veins. "Why not? Jo's great."

"Hmph. She made inappropriate drawings."

Oh. Ah Ma was still upset about the dick pic.

"I thought it was hilarious," Dad said. "Though your mother and I would have won if Jo hadn't drawn such a clear picture of a *shaft*."

"Enough," Zach said. "I'm actually here to see Ah Yeh."

At that, Ah Yeh walked into the front hall. "What is it?"

"I want to learn how to make ginger beef. It's Jo's favorite, and I want to ask her to be with me. For real."

Some part of him protested, reminding him of all the ways this could go wrong.

But he needed to do this. For Jo. And for himself.

"I will help you," Ah Yeh said, "but first you need to go to the grocery store to get a few things."

Zach returned half an hour later with the ingredients, along with flowers for his mother and grandmother. He'd also brought his family a few foods in Toronto that couldn't be found here. Asian eggplants and gai lan, for example.

His parents and grandparents were already in the kitchen.

"Stuart has convinced me that Jo will be good for you," Ah Ma said, "even if she draws inappropriate things if front of your family. I give you my blessing."

"Thank you," Zach said.

"Me, too," Mom said. "I was worried you wouldn't let yourself fall in love again after Marianne. I'm glad I was wrong."

"No, you were right. That's what I thought until recently. But this crept up on me, and Nick, Greg, Tasha, and Lily talked some sense into me."

"Now start cooking," Ah Ma said. "I want to see you cook."

"Is everyone going to watch?" Zach asked. "And provide unwanted comments?"

"I'm afraid so," Dad said.

"It's not a cooking competition." That, of course, didn't deter Zach's family, and Zach understood. He'd had a good time watching Nick bake for Lily last year.

He sighed.

Oh, well. Jo was worth it.

He owed her something special, that was for sure.

Chapter 12

Jo plodded down the sidewalk toward Zach's house. He'd texted, asking her to come over, and here she was.

Perhaps he wanted to make up for last night. Yeah, that was probably it.

But she had plans of her own. She would do what she should have done last week: tell him they needed to stop their Friday nights together at Finn's.

She wasn't sure what kind of excuse she'd use. She didn't want to reveal her feelings. Maybe she'd just say that having sex had made things weird between them?

She couldn't help recalling how it had felt when he dove between her legs and licked her, when he slid inside her... He'd made her feel beautiful again, after Matt had made her feel like she wasn't worth his time. She was thankful for that.

But this had to end.

·❤·❤·❤·❤·❤·

All of the food was ready.

The ginger beef Zach had cooked with his grandfather hadn't made it home. He hadn't expected it to. He'd let his family consume it, then made a new batch back at his place, as well as gai lan with oyster sauce and some rice. He also had drinks and dessert.

Now he was waiting. He couldn't remember the last time he'd been this nervous, but he was going to declare his feelings for the woman he loved, and he couldn't help it. He just hoped she was interested and it wasn't too late.

He was so nervous that he started reciting the periodic table as he paced the hallway, and then, when he was at silicon—atomic number fourteen—his doorbell rang.

Jo curled her hands into fists, ready to do battle.

But when Zach opened the door, she lost her nerve. An errant lock of hair flopped over his forehead, as it often did, and she itched to touch it. He was wearing jeans and a gray Henley, and dammit, she wanted to pull off his shirt again, but she wouldn't.

She had a mission, and she would not fail.

"I have something to tell you," they both said at exactly the same time.

This was followed by synchronized awkward laughs.

"Let me go first," Zach said.

She nodded. She could delay this another minute or two.

He took her hand and led her into the kitchen. It smelled good in here. There were utensils and empty plates set out on the kitchen table, as well as a vase of mini carnations.

No, she must not let her resolve waver. She'd say her piece, then go home and eat Kraft Dinner rather than whatever he'd planned here. He probably wanted to get her in bed, and as appealing as that sounded, she wouldn't let herself do it again.

But if he just wanted sex, would he have done all this?

She told herself not to get hopeful.

"We're going to play a round of Pictionary." Zach walked to the whiteboard in the corner of the kitchen. The same one that had been at his parents' house.

"Okay." She sat down. She had no idea where he was going with this, but she could give him one round of Pictionary.

He picked up a marker and started drawing. It was pretty clear what it was.

"Eye," she said.

He nodded, then drew something else.

A heart.

Her pulse kicked up a notch.

Lastly, he drew an animal. It was fluffy—a sheep?

"Eye love sheep," she said, even though she was pretty sure it meant something else. But that seemed too good to be true.

He shook his head and held her gaze.

She swallowed.

"Eye love ewe," she whispered.

"Point for Team Hipster." He knelt in front of her, taking her hands in his. "I never thought I'd want this again. I was heartbroken after Marianne left, but there was a good side to the break-up. I found a friend in you. Some people assume the events of life just roll right off me. But you didn't assume that. You understood what I was going through, and you helped me get past it without every Friday night turning into a misery fest. Our nights together were the highlight of my week."

This was really happening. It was an effort for Jo to keep breathing.

Eye love ewe. I love you.

"I said I'd never have another relationship," Zach continued, "because I was afraid of being hurt again. But I've been over my ex for a long time, and I think I was holding onto it because I felt like our friendship depended on us both being single and heartbroken." He squeezed her hands. "I was wrong. And as we went out for dinner and skated hand in hand and won Pictionary because of your incredible drawing skills..."

Jo couldn't help blushing.

"...I realized our friendship was changing. I still want to be your friend, of course, but I want something else, too, though it took a while for me to accept it. I think you may have felt that way about me for a long time—much longer than the past month—but never said anything because you thought it was hopeless. I'm sorry, Jo, for not seeing what we could be for each other until recently, but I do now, and the last month has been the best of my life. You're beautiful, sexy, intelligent, kind, and you have a huge competitive spirit hidden beneath it all."

She chuckled, but at the same time, tears came to her eyes. She was overwhelmed.

"It's been a long time for me," she said hoarsely. "Two years."

"We have a lot to make up for." He wiped away the lone tear that had fallen from the corner of her eye, but he didn't tell her not to cry.

Instead, he walked to the counter and dished out some rice, then—oh my God!

"You made ginger beef!" she exclaimed.

"I had my grandfather teach me, while the rest of my family watched, unfortunately."

"Did they hear the gossip about our fake relationship?"

"They did."

"I'm sorry. I was at the bakery with Tiffany—she's the only one I confided in—and Shelly Sanderson overheard. I was telling Tiffany that I had to let you go."

"And now?" He came to stand in front of her.

"You want this to be real, and there's nothing I'd like more."

She stood up and threw her arms around him. He pulled her close, and then his lips were on hers, tender and needy at the same time. He slipped his hands under her sweater and stroked her skin as he kissed her. Kisses that were full of love.

"I love you," she murmured. "I never thought I'd actually say that to you, but I do."

"And I love you. I was just too stupid to realize it until recently."

"Not stupid. You weren't ready, but you are now, and you were worth the wait."

"Is that so?" He cocked an eyebrow, then pressed himself against her, the winning word from the infamous Pictionary game between her legs.

"Let's eat first," she said.

"Good idea." He returned to the counter to dish out the rest of the ginger beef, followed by a green vegetable. "Gai lan with oyster sauce. I know you like broccoli, so you'll probably enjoy it."

She was sure she would.

He brought over their plates of food, then returned to the fridge. Before sitting down, he placed two bottles of Guinness on the table.

She laughed. "You're drinking Guinness, too? You don't like it."

"Just for today, since it's your favorite." He raised his bottle and clinked it against hers. "Cheers."

As they ate their food—Zach had done an excellent job cooking—they held hands under the table and gave each other dopey looks, and occasionally exchanged a few words. He told her about his trip to Toronto to see his brothers.

"Next time you can come with me," he said, and she grinned, still unable to believe this was happening.

After they finished their dinner, he asked her to close her eyes.

When he set his hands on her shoulders a minute later and told her to open her eyes, there was a giant sundae on the table.

"Are these the fudge brownies from Cardinal's?"

"They are, and there aren't any children to knock it onto the floor. And since we're in the privacy of my home..."

Zach sat down next to her. He dipped a spoon into the ice cream covered in chocolate sauce and held it up to her mouth. She wrapped her lips around the spoon and ate the ice cream, then licked her lips, nice and slow, relishing the desire in his eyes.

Next, she fed him a bite of fudge brownie with ice cream, and he did the same thing, his tongue swirling over his lips in slow motion.

She shifted in her seat before standing up. "My turn to draw."

She didn't erase his "eye heart ewe" but drew another picture at the bottom of the whiteboard. Two stick figures, the one with long hair lying on top of the other. She added a large rectangle—the bed—and a smaller rectangle under one of the stick figure's heads. A pillow.

"Ooh," Zach said. "I know this. Group push-ups? Calisthenics? Surfboarding?"

"That's an odd way to surfboard."

He shrugged before giving her a lopsided smile that suffused her with joy and warmth.

She no longer had to hide how she felt about him.

She'd already had much of what she wanted in her life, but now she had the one person she'd assumed would never return her feelings.

Fortunately, she'd been wrong.

They finished eating the sundae before going upstairs so she could show him *exactly* what those two stick figures were doing in her drawing.

Epilogue

It had been a while since Zach Wong had gone out with a woman on Valentine's Day.

He'd left school right after classes ended, and he and Jo had driven up north to the skating trail, which had been full of couples.

Now the two of them were having dinner at Cardinal's, sitting at the same table where they'd had their first "date" a month ago. Zach was having the lamb; Jo had ordered the eggplant parmesan. She was wearing a sweater that showed a tantalizing amount of cleavage, and her hair fell in soft waves about her face.

How had it taken him so long to realize how beautiful she was?

He was very glad he'd decided to get a fake girlfriend for Chinese New Year, and even happier that he had a real girlfriend for Valentine's Day.

"I don't know why they're out together for Valentine's," said a woman standing near the door. "Everyone knows their relationship is fake. What's the point in pretending now?"

Across from him, Jo stifled a laugh.

"I heard the whole fake relationship story was actually a lie," another woman said.

"Then how did the rumor start?"

"Shelly overheard Jo MacGregor talking to Tiffany Bauer, but maybe Jo was being sarcastic. Shelly's not always great with sarcasm."

The women headed outside, and their voices faded into the night.

"Well," Zach said, "we gave everyone in town a lot to talk about."

"We certainly did," Jo said.

For dessert, they ordered a fudge brownie sundae. Sure, they'd shared one of these just six days ago, but it was a special occasion.

Although Zach hadn't celebrated Valentine's Day in years, he knew he'd be celebrating it again next year with the woman sitting across from him. They hadn't been together for long, but somehow, he just knew.

She slipped a spoonful of ice cream into her mouth and swirled her tongue around it.

Okay, that was it. Time to get out of here.

But before he could ask for the bill, his mother walked toward him, followed by his dad.

"We didn't think you'd be here," Mom said. "We figured you'd stay in for your first Valentine's Day."

Zach shouldn't be surprised. This was the thing about living in a town where there was only one "nice" restaurant: you were bound to run into lots of people you knew when you were out for Valentine's Day. Including your parents.

Still, he wouldn't trade this life for anything.

"Hi, Jo," Dad said. "Nice to see you doing something other than drawing phallic objects."

Jo choked on her ice cream.

Just then, Zach's phone rang. It was his grandparents. Shit, why were they calling at eight thirty? Was everything okay?

"Zach," Ah Ma said when he answered the phone. "You have been lying to us again."

"What have I been lying about?"

"Silly boy. You know! Sebastian and Amber were together, and you didn't tell me?"

"Wasn't my news to share."

"Of course it was. You hear news like that, you immediately tell your ah ma."

Zach pulled the phone away from his ear. His grandmother was too loud.

"It's Ah Ma," he said to his parents. "Since she's probably going to call you next, you might as well know that Sebastian and Amber are seeing each other, and yes, I already knew, but was sworn to secrecy. For obvious reasons."

"*Were* seeing each other," Ah Ma said. "I think they have broken up now, but I don't know, because nobody tells me anything. *You* didn't tell me your girlfriend was fake."

"That would have defeated the purpose of the fake relationship."

Dad grabbed the phone and said something to his mother in Cantonese, then ended the call and handed the phone back to Zach.

"Anyway," Mom said, "we'll deal with that tomorrow. You two have a nice night."

His parents headed to a table at the far end of the restaurant, and Zach took Jo's hand as they finished off their ice cream sundae.

"Sorry about the interruption," he said.

"No problem." She was laughing.

After he paid the bill, they headed out into the snowy night. She pressed a quick kiss to his mouth, snowflakes in her lashes, and they started back to his house, where they would do something more fun than play Pictionary. No beer at Finn's tonight—he had other plans.

"Hi, Mr. Wong! Dr. MacGregor!" said one of Zach's super-keen grade ten students.

Zach lifted a hand in response.

He kept his arm around Jo's waist as they walked through the familiar streets of Mosquito Bay. This was their home, and they belonged here.

Together.

About the Author

Jackie Lau decided she wanted to be a writer when she was in grade two, sometime between writing "The Heart That Got Lost" and "The Land of Shapes." She later studied engineering and worked as a geophysicist before turning to writing romance novels. Jackie lives in Toronto with her husband, and despite living in Canada her whole life, she hates winter. When she's not writing, she enjoys gelato, gourmet donuts, cooking, hiking, and reading on the balcony when it's raining.

To learn more and sign up for her newsletter,
visit jackielaubooks.com.

Also by Jackie Lau

Love, Lies, and Cherry Pie

Donut Fall in Love Series
Donut Fall in Love
The Stand-Up Groomsman

Weddings with the Moks Series
Four Weddings to Fall in Love
Three Reasons to Run

Chu's Restaurant Series
The Sitcom Star
The Reluctant Heartthrob

Kwan Sisters/Fong Brothers Series

Grumpy Fake Boyfriend

Mr. Hotshot CEO

Pregnant by the Playboy

Bidding for the Bachelor

Cider Bar Sisters Series

Her Big City Neighbor

His Grumpy Childhood Friend

Her Pretend Christmas Date (novella)

The Professor Next Door

Her Favorite Rebound

Her Unexpected Roommate

Holidays with the Wongs Series

A Match Made for Thanksgiving

A Second Chance Road Trip for Christmas

A Fake Girlfriend for Chinese New Year

A Big Surprise for Valentine's Day

Baldwin Village Series

One Bed for Christmas (prequel novella)

The Ultimate Pi Day Party

Ice Cream Lover

Man vs. Durian

Chin-Williams Series

Not Another Family Wedding

He's Not My Boyfriend